P9-CBQ-824

The Immaculate Conception Photography Gallery

and other stories

Katherine Govier

Little, Brown and Company (Canada) Limited
Boston • Toronto • London

Canadian Cataloguing in Publication Data

Govier, Katherine, 1948–
        The immaculate conception photography
gallery and other stories

ISBN 0–316–31984–8

I. Title

PS8563.0875155 1994   C813'.54   C94–931688–1
PR9199.3C68155 1994

Cover artwork: Linda Montgomery
Cover design: Tania Craan
Interior design and typesetting: Pixel Graphics
Printed and bound in Canada by Best Gagné Print-
ing Inc.

Little, Brown and Company (Canada) Limited
148 Yorkville Avenue, Toronto, Ontario

For John, Robin and Emily

Acknowledgements

The author thanks Kim McArthur, Janet Harron and the staff of Little, Brown Canada for their enthusiastic work on this volume. Greg Ioannou's keen editing was also much appreciated.

The stories included here are all works of fiction: resemblance to living persons is entirely accidental.

"Aliens" first appeared in a slightly different form in *Discovery* Magazine (Hong Kong).

"Learning to Swim" first appeared in *Enroute* (Toronto).

"The Immaculate Conception Photography Gallery" was a winner of the CBC Literary Contest in 1989, was broadcast on CBC Radio's "Speaking Volumes, and also appeared in *Saturday Night* Magazine.

"The Immaculate Conception Baby Shower" and "The Immaculate Conception Photography Gallery" were dramatized for CBC Radio's "Morningside" for broadcast in the fall of 1994.

Table of Contents

The Immaculate
Conception
Baby Shower

When Sarah Stafford's engagement to Chip Cunningham was called off, Sarah showed unnatural spunk and announced that she was going to Dawson City to work as a can-can dancer at Diamond Tooth Gertie's.

Pearl Stafford was aghast.

"You can't possibly. Way up there? In a place like that the only reason they even have women is to serve men's pleasure." Her voice was gravelly and her throat tendons twitched.

"You've never even been there, Mother."

Sarah hadn't either, not yet, but she was in a hurry to go. She was packing her dance leotards and the large rubber boots that had been recommended, because spring came late and the snow was still melting in mid-May. Sarah's was one of those Calgary families with a ranch south of town where the Royal Family made stop offs whenever any of them were in the vicinity, a seat on the

Stampede Board, and a barn full of cutting horses. Sarah was not horsy. Furthermore, on June 21 her older sister Janet would marry Norm Grisdale. With her own wedding no longer in the offing, Sarah did not wish to attend. Not that she was jealous: Norm was a man of no particular distinction; in fact, the Judge had asked him in jest if he wanted to change his last name to Stafford.

In Dawson Sarah met a placer miner named Pete Gilhooley. His family had its stake up in the hills half an hour's drive east. He was brown-skinned and muscular with a sharp nose, high cheekbones and level, peat-brown eyes. Diagonally across his forehead fell a lock of straight hair, which he threw off by tossing his head. Pete had grown up riding bareback over the moss and rocks, and did school by correspondence until he was fifteen, when he was sent out to Vancouver. But he never liked the south, and when his Dad died he came back to take over the mine. It was still a one-man operation. Pete dug and sifted for gold all summer and in fall he flew out with the nuggets. It gave him enough money to spend the darkest part of the winter in Hawaii.

The ice had just broken up when Sarah arrived. No one slept—they'd slept through the darkness of October through May— least of all the lovers. Sarah and Pete made love in the sunlit midnights all summer long; by August Chip Cunningham was nothing but a blip on the screen. The tourists decamped Dawson and in September Sarah brought Pete down to Priddis. Janet, who'd made a swift journey from bride to matron, and Norm came for Sunday brunch to meet Sarah's boyfriend. Pearl Stafford made a steak and kidney pie.

The pastry steaming on her plate, Pearl pushed her elbows out of their silk swathing and up on the table. "So Peter, tell me, who are your people?"

Sarah had taken Pete out the day before to get him a pale blue button-down shirt and a pair of grey flannels; he balked at the blazer and had rolled up his shirt-sleeves.

"They've been in Dawson since the nineties," said Pete in his soft voice. "I don't think you'd know them. My mother was Milly—"

"I can't hear what he is saying, can you?" trumpeted the Judge, who suffered a selective deafness. Pearl smiled in a glacial way at Pete. Perhaps she was thinking of his pleasure, to which she imagined the entire female population of Dawson was dedicated.

"Now exactly where *is* the Yukon? I could never quite make out. West of here, or straight overhead, what do they say in *Peter Pan*? 'Straight on 'till morning?' Do you know the Woodwards? The Siftons? Dear Effie is so sweet. The last time I was in Palm Springs she leant me her car and driver— Ernest, isn't that his name?—for the entire day."

"You can't take mother *seriously*," Sarah whispered when she sneaked into the guest room to visit Pete. She advised him to make a joke of it. "I don't know the Siftons but Ernest is a good guy," would have done, for instance. But Pete was not to be patronized. Love lost its sweetness in the longer dark of southern Alberta. Two more days and they had a violent quarrel under Pearl's smiling eyes. "You're somebody else down here," said Pete."It's like I don't even know you." The visit was a failure. Pete withdrew to the north alone and Sarah betrayed not a whisper of pain.

"Sarah is such a wit," her brother Michael said after. "She went out and found herself an *actual* gold digger." It was a good line, and so often repeated that eventually Sarah herself began to use it.

When Sarah Stafford was approaching forty, and still unmarried, Pearl fretted. A husband was no longer the issue. The issue was issue. At this point marriage was too long and too unreliable a route. In the sitting room Pearl laid down her copy of *Woman's Journal*, airmailed from England.

"You know you don't have to forgo the greatest of life's joys, just because you're not married," she said to her daughter's sturdy profile.

Sarah continued to look out the window. She was a lawyer in the family firm. She was heavier, her can-can days long over. Her profile sat well at a board table. Her hair was twisted into an elegant but tight knot at the nape of her neck. Her cheek reflected the cool spring light on melting snow. Men had dared to woo her but none had succeeded. From time to time people brought up that dreadful Pete Gilhooley. Something in that incident troubled Pearl. She tumbled it in her mind, as if she could unlock it, learn a secret about Sarah. But it produced nothing and she tossed it aside.

She had known that seeing the children into proper marriages would not be easy, with the ranch to think of, the Windermere property, the trust, the shares in the old firm. Janet of course had Norm, who was now one of them, more suitable than Janet, really.

The Stafford family was what was known as close. The word "close" has a number of meanings: close as in tight with money; close as in hot and stuffy, like a small room; close as in loving and intimate. Some of these meanings applied; it depended on who you talked to. It was a family of means and a certain tradition: comfortably wealthy to the point where greed need not be displayed, but could be satisfied regularly by the clipping of coupons. One of them had made the money one hundred years ago floating frozen cattle carcasses down the river. Stafford power was limited to the Stampede Board now, their influence likewise: in the Calgary establishment ranchers had been upstaged by daring oilmen, and oilmen by foxy bureaucrats. Staffords appeared not to notice. Without going so far as to claim eccentricity, they valued wit, intelligence and independence. Position assured and nothing to prove, they felt free to do as they pleased.

"Sarah, this is the end of the twentieth century," Pearl went on, in a nettling vein. "There have got to be some aspects of progress of which you can take advantage. When a woman wishes to become pregnant she has options."

The sun streamed in, making Sarah pale. "I realize that," she said dryly. "Shall we go through them? One. Ask a male friend. I won't. Presumably if any of them wanted to, they'd have asked me themselves."

"I don't know that you can necessarily assume that," countered Pearl. "They might not have thought—" Sarah interrupted her.

"Two. Utilize a stranger, with or without permission," Sarah hurried on, over her mother. "I could pick my day, let my hair down, find a man in a bar on Electric Avenue and get on with it."

Pearly winced, as she was meant to.

"You see, I *have* thought it through. I don't relish the thought of picking somebody up. How many times would I have to try? Moreover even the most attractive, virus-free stranger has all those unknown genes. Dyspepsia, thick ankles, who knows? No, mother, a friend would never do, and a stranger is out of the question."

"But my dear, there are *clinics*. You go, you sign up, and you have a choice of race, colouring, educational background and creed. The donors are all medical students, so you knew they're not stupid."

Sarah really did long for a baby. To run home from work to, to smell its tiny head, to mould, to cling to. Pearl was persuasive and Sarah found herself with her mother at a clinic. It was like getting a massage, easy and impersonal. They were discriminating shoppers. "How long has this been frozen?" they asked. "Is there a best-before date?" Sarah went through it three times, with Pearl at her side. But she did not get pregnant.

By then another summer had come around.

Sarah told her mother she was going to give up. At Windermere, she and Janet lay on their backs on the dock, arms folded over their faces. They were closer now, Sarah's natural advantages lessening with age, and Janet's contentment making her too lazy to be envious. Janet's boys, nine and fourteen, were on the raft, splashing and shouting and pushing each other off into the water. Janet's body had an attractive used quality, with a little cellulite around the thighs. Sarah peered down at her sister's complacent belly, the pelvic bones that rose on either side of it like little horns. A stab of envy, coupled with a visceral hunger to grow a baby, went through Sarah. She got up on her elbow.

"Listen, Janet, why don't you let me use Norm?"

They all knew what Sarah was going through.

"You mean, for the baby?"

Sarah nodded.

Janet pressed her lips down in a quizzical expression; her eyebrows went up. She didn't think long. She climbed the steps and found Norm in the kitchen pouring the G and T's. Norm had no trouble with it. In half an hour Janet came back down to the dock and said to her sister, "It's a go." It seemed the charitable thing to do.

When Sarah got pregnant she told everyone it was artificial insemination. She had always been forthright. Instantly, in a way that suggested it had always been their idea, the Staffords pledged unconditional support. Old friends escorted Sarah to public events throughout her happy pregnancy. The project seemed to suit her; the attention enlivened her face. Long-dormant dramatic instincts emerged when she called the family to her lying-in bed for an announcement. Highly coloured, magnificently big-bellied, she leaned back on eyelet-trimmed pillows in the old brass bed, her hands folded on the counterpane.

"I would like my parents to know the father," said Sarah. Her eyes went to Norm, standing at the foot of the bed, his hair receding from an unlined, almost clerical countenance. "The father is my brother-in-law Norm." In the ensuing silence she continued to speak. For six months after she would stay home with the child, while continuing her work part-time. The secretary would come to her bedside; the nanny would stand by.

Afterward there was a slight milling, if one can mill in a bedroom, and awkward chuckling and shaking of hands. Janet stayed alone by the fireplace. She wished Sarah had said "donor" and not "father." She had not liked the look that crossed from Sarah to Norm. Belatedly, it seemed to her they had entered into a conspiracy, its consummation to be this child. She had pitied Sarah. After all, she, Janet, had never been jilted by the likes of Chip Cunningham. And *her* passion at twenty had been for this young man who was discreet and well-shod and manageable. There was a time when the family turned up its nose at Norm. But Norm had proven himself suitable. He was one of them now. In fact he was two of them — Janet's husband, and

Sarah's child's father.

Pity was appropriate. Jealousy was not. Maybe she felt this way because Sarah talked about *her* job, *her* nanny, *her* secretary, *her* child. The woman who had everything. Until now, they'd neatly divided the arena. Janet was a wife and mother, Sarah was a lawyer. But now Sarah had strayed into Janet's territory; she had strayed in, borrowed the bull, and determined to live in both halves from now on. Janet realized too late that she was against this idea of a child for Sarah. A little aphorism of her mother's ran through her mind: *You don't get your second choice too.*

People came to call. The beautiful fat-cheeked babe was admired. Sarah was commanding with her swollen breasts under her bedjacket, and her legal briefs, scattered on the counterpane. She was in her element. Not since she went up to Dawson had her originality been so remarked upon. As little Alice Jane Stafford slumbered in her bassinet, her story became dinner-table *bruit* from Mount Royal to Bragg Creek.

"You have to know the Staffords. They're very close."

"And getting closer!"

"I don't blame her for doing it, but why on earth didn't she get a stranger?"

"They like to keep it in the family."

Some defended Sarah.

"Why shouldn't she go ahead on her own? I'd have done it, if it were my last chance!"

Others were bitter.

"You'd all do it if you could. Dispense with husbands all together."

They split hairs.

"I have no problem with her getting a sperm donor. But the brother-in-law?"

They developed theories.

"It's so WASP. So anti-passion—"

"—so Canadian—"

"—a purely pragmatic solution to an emotional need."

They predicted dire consequences.

"It will end in a mess, wait and see. They're acting as if this was a business deal—"

"There must be contracts. Never fear. They'll have had it lawyered. "

"Is anyone thinking of the kid?"

"Wait 'till they start fighting! The transcripts of the court case will be to die for."

"Well, *is* anyone thinking of the kid? Lucky it wasn't a boy."

"I don't know why you'd say that. What earthly difference does it—

Various biases were revealed.

"The Staffords think they can legislate feelings. Think of the father! Thanksgiving and Christmas dinners, this other child will be there."

"Norm won't take a role."

"How can he not? It's his child."

"Well at least it's not a boy. Boys need their—"

"Countless men never take a role with their children, boy or girl."

"Who says?"

"It's common knowledge."

And blame was laid.

"If you ask me it all goes back to the mother. You have to know Pearl."

"It all goes back to Chip Cunningham."

"Sarah never had any sense about men. Do you remember that gold panner from the Yukon, and how the family chased him away?"

Curiously, as she had promoted the idea, Pearl was having more trouble with Sarah's announcement about the donor than anyone. "Whatever do you think can have caused Sarah's profound rejection of men?" she rather cunningly asked her husband.

"I doubt it's a rejection of anyone. Perhaps she prefers total control to unpredictable involvements with people of the opposite sex," said the Judge.

"Isn't that the kind of shortcut we'd all love to take?" said Pearl, becoming sententious. "My generation always thought that the penalty for having children was having to take on some man as well. And all the risk that entails. "

"What do you mean by that?" said the Judge.

Pearl pursed her lips. "Not to mention loss of control."

"I know what your problem is!" crowed the Judge suddenly. "You're jealous! You've had to put up with marriage to me! She's running her own show and now she can produce an heir, too.

Furthermore, she's been public about it, and you do nothing but fret about what people think."

As all this was being said, Sarah's friends began to rally. They were mostly men, at the office—lawyers she'd trained with and who were her lunch partners, and a few secretaries. They decided to have a shower for Sarah.

It was fall. The condo belonging to her friend Michael was decorated with gourds and cattails from the market, and pots of chrysanthemums from the flower shop on Mount Royal Avenue. The guests came bearing their gifts, and Sarah sat in the pine rocker, which Michael festooned with the curly tear-offs from the edges of his computer paper. Norm and Janet stayed away.

The men were uncomfortable at first, looking out the windows and talking business. Michael clapped his hands in the centre of the room, calling them to order. "Come! Gather round!" Only a handful sat in the circle while Sarah opened the gifts. But Chip Cunningham had a pad of paper, and kept a list of who gave what, while Geoff went around the floor picking up the crumpled paper. Michael passed the gifts after she had opened them. Soon they relaxed and began examining the layette items, talking about feeding schedules.

They were down to the last two presents when Pearl swept in with Alice swaddled in a pink hand-crocheted blanket. She handed her to Sarah, who turned her classic profile to the little squashed face, and grasped the tiny clenched fist.

"It's changed her," the men began to say. "She's softer."

"Taken off weight, too."

Pearl was over the worst: she had faced her canasta club, told them straight out, after practising in the mirror first. You just had to banish shame; her husband was right. Staffords ought never to worry about what people thought. Besides, everyone could see the sense of it.

Now, watching the young people at the shower, she felt not unhappy. Look at all these men. Sarah's friends were over forty. The starter marriages were long over. There had been divorces, soon there would be widowers too. It was not too late.

Sarah Stafford sat in her rocking throne, perforated paper curls on either side of her shoulders. She was dazzled by the brightness of her baby, by her own miraculous creation. It was as if a faraway light shone on them both. I am some anomalous transitional being, she thought. My brain is dense with information. The whole of my child's future lives in there, miniaturized, waiting to be exploded.

Oh, Alice, she swore to the bundle in her lap. I will be a good mother. I shall try to do this exactly right. When you're twelve I'll make an announcement—Uncle Norm is your father, your cousins are your sister and brother. You'll be sad, no doubt, to settle for Norm, but then so was I. You'll have wanted a father, but certainly not him, who will seem even less like a father than he did when he was an uncle. It will be like getting money for a birthday present—no fun because no one took a risk. You can't complain, but still you feel cheated.

Alice, you'll think it's not fair. Not fair to be the descendent of a single person, to be growing straight downward in a line on the family tree, only one branch making you, and that branch your mother's will. Not fair to be conceived of determination alone, to be a product of your mother's desire to reproduce herself.

You'll be furious at your perfect indivisible parent, and Alice, where will you turn? Children of divorce have an option, the other parent, orphans, at least a memory. You will have no one. What did Jesus do when he was a teenager?

You will reject the idea of Norm as your father. What is a father, after all? Someone who gave seed. No, Norm isn't one, any more than the farmer who eats a plum and throws the pit on a fertile mound is the father of a plum tree. Your father is someone who touched your mother.

I'll tell her about Pete Gilhooley, she thought. We'll have so many years together, to talk. I can see Alice at twenty; she and I will drive to Whitehorse with a canoe on the car. I've never been back. We'll paddle down the river to Dawson.

Alice will love the Yukon, the insistent clear skies, still light at eleven o'clock at night, the feeling of possibility they lend to a day. She will love the undivided boreal forest, where the tree roots knit together in the shallow ground and the tops shoot up for light, thin and close as the teeth of a comb.

In Dawson the board sidewalks are glazed with speckled frost; by noon the sun is hot enough for shirt-sleeves. A man will be on a ladder painting the greyish wooden houses. It will be Pete, or Pete's son, or whatever Pete-equivalent will be abroad in the year 2012. The houses are cardboard boxes, set on the flat gravel base of the town, their false fronts old and touchingly ephemeral, like Calgary used to be. He will have painted half the town, turning it to a candy-scape—red, forest green, blue and white, bright yellow. The other half is the pulpy-grey shade of a new colouring book.

"I love that red," Alice will call up to him.

He'll put down his roller, and climb down to meet her.

They were all clapping at the shower, and calling speech! speech! and wanting Sarah to stand up. She didn't think she'd bother to explain any of that. She looked over at her mother, whose face was stiff and unreadable as a pin-cushion and whose hands shredded a paper napkin deliberately, ferociously. Then she stood and, raising her baby over her head, began to turn, slowly, in Alice's small wrapped shadow.

The Red Queen

Pat opened the door. The children's voices were birdsong. She smiled. Behind the desk, Brenda had two children pulling her by the hand.

"I've come to pick up a girl," said Pat.

"Which one?"

"That one," said Pat, pointing to Jessica. Jessica with curly red hair in a ponytail on top of her head, very small blue jeans and a sweatshirt with panda bears on it. Jessica peeking around the door of the block room at the woman who said her name.

The two children succeeded in removing Brenda from her post; she was dragged across the floor to the cushions where they set about tickling her. Pat slipped around the desk to the block room where Jessica had withdrawn, caught her hand firmly in hers, and walked out. They headed down the echoey hall of the community centre toward the heavy steel doors.

They passed the door to the pool, its chlorine smell. They passed the library window; through it Pat could see the dark-skinned cleaner who let her look at magazines when it was cold.

"I don't have my coat," said Jessica.

"You don't need it," said Pat. "We're going to my house."

"Why?" said Jessica. Pat tightened her grip on Jessica's hand.

"Because I am going to give you tea."

"Oh," said Jessica, retreating under the heavy tone. "Will my mummy be coming to get me at your house then?"

Pat hadn't thought of answers to these questions. She hadn't pictured, when she pictured this, that the child would ask questions. Just that she would sip her tea, and giggle. Her bright face would be sunshine in Pat's room.

"It's just around the corner." And it was. The agency found Pat this room, upstairs in a house on King Street. The house had a Mac's Milk in the main floor, and a beauty parlour on the second. Pat's bedsit was an old sunporch stuck out the back. It was close to the community centre where there was, the social worker said, "so much to do!"; with the store downstairs, Pat could be independent.

Pat didn't remember how long ago she'd moved into the room. By now she knew Iqbal in the milk store and Betty in the beauty parlour. Betty even did her hair once. Pat sat in the red leather chair, and looked at herself in the mirror. Of course the woman staring back was not really her. Staring back was a thick warty pig of a woman with glasses

that magnified her eyes. The real Pat was bubbly
and blonde-pretty with a smooth peach blush.

Pat wondered where Miss Piggy came
from. The hospital? Or did she take over after,
when Pat moved here and had to take the pills? The
social worker came once a week. Maybe it had been
years and years and now she was old. But she
didn't think so.

"Do you know my mummy?" Jessica challenged.

"Of course I do," said Pat. She held Jessica
with one hand while she scrounged in her purse
with the other for her key.

"We have to be quiet going in, because people work here," she said, opening the door.

Jessica gazed up the steps. There were
signs with arrows going left. There was no arrow to
the way they were going.

The girl stood in the centre of the floor with her
legs apart and her arms folded over the pandas on
her sweat shirt. "I think you were bad to bring me
here."

Pat smiled, to show her pretty even teeth,
and flicked back the wave of shiny blonde hair that
fell across her cheek. This was the dream. Home
from shopping with her darling child! You toss
your shopping bags on the sofa and flounce down
after them, laughing. A tray of tea and cookies carried in. Pat had nothing to throw down on the
couch so she threw herself. Because she was short-

legged and heavy, she landed with a plop on the edge of the worn sofa bed.

"How can you say bad? Oh, don't spoil my fun, don't spoil it. We're just going to have tea!"

Jessica cheered up. She knew how to play. "Okay!" she said. "We're going to have tea. And you're the mummy?"

"I'm the mummy and you're the little girl and we've just been out shopping. Daddy's still at work wouldn't you know—and we've got time before we have to make dinner."

Jessica skipped around the room. "You make the tea and I'll set the table!" She pulled a chair away from the wall, and then the old hassock.

"We need a table!"

Pat brought out the wooden carton she kept her records in and turned it over.

"We need a table cloth!"

Pat ran to her drawers and found the extra pillow case. The social worker had given her two sets of sheets and told her to remember to wash one set every week.

"Here!"

Jessica spread it over the crate. "Now you have to put the kettle on."

At the day care Brenda wept.

"You-had-never-seen-this-woman-before?" said the supervisor, her words like steady blows. "Yet you let her take Jessica?"

"She looked familiar. I thought she was a babysitter."

The children had been collected. Only Andrew and Milo remained, fighting over a dump-truck. After closing time parents were billed a dollar a minute. Andrew's and Milo's parents ran up big bills. Jessica's father, pale as play dough, stood in the hallway talking to a policeman.

"She did look familiar," piped up Anthoula, who was only part-time. "She's around here a lot, in front of the library." No one listened.

The supervisor became rhetorical. "How many times have we gone over the rules? You never let a child go except with a parent unless we've had a phone call."

"I did phone Jessica's father," said Brenda.

"*After* you let her go." The supervisor turned away in disgust. Andrew turned up at Brenda's knee. "Are you mad at Jessica? Are you mad?" he said, tugging her hand.

Brenda sobbed again.

"**O**h *no*!" cried Pat, in her dream voice. "I forgot the milk!"

"You don't have any milk?" said Jessica. "Maybe I should go home then." She was tired and hungry. Usually after daycare she had a snack.

Pat's face was dogged. "You're not going home. We haven't had tea."

"Do I know you?" said Jessica, suddenly.

Pat flashed the beautiful mother smile, and plumped up the cushion behind her.

"Remember I told you how convenient this room was? Guess what? The milk store is just downstairs!" She hadn't known she would remember what the social worker said to her, but it came back now. "All we have to do is go out, locking the door behind us, and then walk down the stairs, around the corner, and in to the front of the house. And that milk store is open all day and all night too! My friend Iqbal works there."

She took Jessica firmly by the hand. They clattered down the stairs, heedless now, of the noise.

"Who's Iqbal?" said Jessica.

Pat opened the street door. The sun was setting at the far end of King Street. The sky was in swirls of orange and grey. The street lights were round and hazy. Pat called them hospital moons because they were like the lights she used to see when she woke up after her treatment. She was happy when she saw them, because she knew it would be a whole week before she had another.

Everyone was walking fast, going home to their people. "It's getting dark," said Jessica. She was afraid. She never went out in the dark. "It's too late for tea."

They were outside Mac's Milk. Pat could see Iqbal inside, behind the counter, selling a lottery ticket. Suddenly she thought that she did not want Iqbal to see Jessica.

"You wait here. I'll go get the milk." She let go of Jessica's hand. Jessica hesitated.

"I'm going home," she said again. But how? Where? Jessica couldn't run away in the dark. She clutched Pat's hand again.

"Take me in with you."

They opened the door. A man pushed past

them out into the street, his lottery ticket clutched in his hand. Iqbal was crouched behind the counter stacking something.

"You have to hide," said Pat. "Stand here. Make sure he doesn't see you."

Jessica stood behind a rack of cereal boxes. She did not move. Pat went to the cold chests and pulled out a carton of milk.

"I'm having a tea party, Iqbal."

"Is this all you need, Pat? Do you have bread?"

But she wanted him to understand. "It's because I'm lonely. I need someone to love."

"I know you're lonely. Have you got your kitten yet? Cats like milk, don't they."

Jessica listened. She thought it was funny how the man talked to Pat. It was not the way clerks talked to other grownups. He acted like Pat was stupid. Jessica stepped out from behind the rack into the aisle. Iqbal did not look up.

"Do you have your money, Pat?"

"Oh, I forgot!" she wheedled.

"You can't keep doing this. The social worker said."

"She'll pay it. She always does."

"I'm not supposed to give you credit. The boss doesn't like it. You don't want me to lose my job, Pat. You don't want me to go away."

Pat whimpered. "I'll remember next time."

"I'm writing it down Pat," said Iqbal.

"Write it down, okay."

At last Iqbal looked up. "Who's that little girl?" he said.

Pat turned her terrible face to Jessica. "I told you to hide!" Iqbal smiled. "Your friend for tea?" he said, and crouched down behind the counter again.

When they opened the door to the bedsit the burner was bright red under the kettle and there was no steam coming out.

"You let it boil dry," said Jessica, whose mother did the same thing. "You need one of those where the button pops out and it turns off."

"Oh?" said Pat, confused. She turned off the burner and picked up the kettle. It burned her hand, so she dropped it. "Ow!"

"Don't touch!" cried Jessica, too late. There was a terrible pause, while Pat hissed over her burnt hand. Jessica pulled herself up tall. "You can't be the mother," said Jessica. "You're too dumb. I'll be the mother." She tied the dishtowel around her waist. "Let's just have milk and cookies."

Pat's face went dark and her lips hung down. Jessica was giving orders.

"Put out two plates. And glasses for milk."

Pat snarled.

"I know who you look like," said Jessica. "The Red Queen."

"The Red Queen?" said Pat. "Who's that?"

"You know, in *Alice in Wonderland*. 'Off with her head! Off with her head!'" Jessica ran from one side of the room to the other. When she reached a wall she banged it with her fist. "Off with her head!"

Pat's face turned purple. "Don't make noise!" she shouted. "I told you be quiet!"

Jessica stopped.

But Pat was angry now. "You can't make noise because—" she couldn't remember why. She picked up a tin of salmon and threw it against the wall. "I invited you here! I invited you! You have to be nice."

Jessica put her thumb in her mouth, which allowed her to think. Pat was too dumb to be the grownup, so Jessica had to be. Now Pat was having a tantrum. At daycare Michael had tantrums. Brenda always made him stop by talking quietly. Sometimes she wrapped his arms across his stomach and held them behind his back, and she sort of hugged him.

She walked up to Pat. Pat was swinging the bag with the milk in it up against the cupboard door. Milk was splattering on the walls. "Be *nice* to Pat!"

"Give me that!" said Jessica. She was quiet, but firm. She held her hand out.

"No," said Pat. "I'm unmanageable. I am antisocial. I am dangerous. I hurt people. So I have to live by myself."

"Give it to me." Jessica kept the hand out.

Pat handed over the milk bag. Jessica decided against the hug because Pat was so big and she smelled bad. "If you go over there and sit down and think about what you've done, I will come and sit beside you," she said.

Pat went quietly and sat down. In a minute Jessica sat beside her. "Let's watch TV," she said.

The daycare centre was closed. Andrew's and Milo's parents' late charges of $5.00 and $10.00 were recorded in the book. Jessica's mother was crying and her father was phoning lawyers. The police had a description of Pat—short heavy-set "ugly" middle-aged woman with brown hair and glasses—but no one remembered seeing her.

Jessica and Pat watched *Polka Dot Door* and then they watched *The Elephant Show*, and sang along. When it finished Jessica stood up. "You didn't even give me tea or cookies or anything," said Jessica. "I want to go home."

"I don't know where you live."

Pat began to rock. She took a pillow in her lap. Her eyes rolled up in her head.

"Then take me back to daycare."

"It's too late to go back to daycare. It's closed. The lights are out."

Jessica thought about that. "My mum and dad will wait for me," she suggested.

"No, they won't," said Pat. "They'll be so mad at you. They've gone away and they will never come back."

Jessica started to cry. She cried for a while. It was very dark outside the window. She could hear cars honking on the street. It was noisier than at home. Suddenly Pat pushed her on the floor.

"Don't!" said Jessica.

Pat leaned down and hit her across the face.

Jessica stood up. She stopped crying. She

knew this was very important. She looked Pat firmly in the eye. "Use your words!" she said. "Not your fists!" But she trembled.

"Oh, you mean Pat," said Jeremy in the library. He had put down his broom and unlocked the sliding glass door. "You're telling me she kidnapped a kid from the daycare?"

Anthoula nodded.

"She's not really smart."

"Has she got a library card? They'll have her address."

"Oh no, I couldn't go looking anything up," said Jeremy. He slid the glass door shut. "We're closed anyway. But that social worker knows where she lives."

It was midnight. A carload of police drew up outside the Mac's Milk. Iqbal looked up scared from behind his counter. They had guns. They might shoot him. But they didn't come in. In the police car he saw the social worker who came in to pay Pat's bills. He hoped they didn't shoot Pat.

He had heard some louder noises than usual from up there tonight. Nobody could stop her temper; she had to wear herself out. But she must have gone to sleep a couple of hours ago because it went quiet. For the first time he thought of the little girl she'd had with her.

He couldn't stand the silence then. He locked the cash and went out the front door, twisting the open sign to closed. When he got to the foot of the stairs he saw Pat come out, dazed, her face damp, the little girl leading her by the hand.

God is Writing a Novel

Tling was an ape who was political. At some risk he had organized demonstrations against his government. On the eve of the round up, when the great mountainside was in flames, he held in his hand a ticket for an American Airlines flight to Toronto. Tling hesitated before boarding. Looking over his shoulder at a peach sky, coconut palms and violet rainclouds, he realized that he might never see his land again. But a hand impelled him through the gate.

Tling arrived safe and free in North America; his friends were shot or went to jail. Reports from Borneo made it clear that Tling must never return.

Ellen was a professor of English, forty years old, ten years divorced. She had cellulite in her thighs, but she was strong and kind, and pretty enough. She met Tling when the Wilsons brought him to the faculty club for Sunday dinner. He was attractive; he was also a *cause célèbre* at the moment. He wore a blue blazer and cheap grey flannels, topsiders on his almost circular feet.

"Tling comes from Borneo," said Rick Wilson. "He's been here six months and he thinks he'll likely stay."

Ellen extended her hand. His eyes were black and deep and sad.

"You like it here, then?" she said.

"I *can't* back to home," said Tling.

"We'll explain later," said Rebecca. Seeing that Tling was looked after, she moved down the bar.

Their handshake grew longer, their feet took root in the floor; Ellen and Tling sensed a portentous moment. Tling twitched. For some time now he had felt he was a plaything of a tyrant. Ellen, on the other hand, felt drawn not only to suffer, but to record. She found Tling easy to talk to. He had so few words and each one was right.

"I lose everything," he said. "Lose language, lose culture, lose power."

Ellen tried to imagine. "I think if it happened to me I would die," she said.

"I feeling that I *am* die," said Tling.

Ellen was shocked. More so when Tling winked at her. A slow, deliberate, seductive wink, signalling intent. She took fright at the implications of it all, turned away and began an animated chat with the man on her right, a psychiatrist who wanted her to join his working group on creativity.

But she backed away, mouthing excuses: essays to mark. Tling's black eyes' soft gleam searched her. She shook his hand again. She produced a card, two cards; she gave him her telephone number, and took his. As she was going out the door, Rick Wilson stopped her. He was one of the scientists who had sponsored Tling. It was his idea to bring him to Toronto.

"He's so unhappy. If there's anything you can do," he said. "He's very fond of music."

Ellen called Tling and invited him to a concert. He inquired as to the type of music. "Classical is good music; pop, rock, I no like," he announced. "Not high class."

"It's Mozart," she said.

Tling agreed to come.

At intermission they chatted in the concert hall foyer. Ellen enjoyed being stared at; she felt comfortable with Tling. She eyed his long body and short legs, and felt a jolt of lust.

"Music good me. No words," he said. "All feeling."

"Yes. Emotions, colour," she agreed. Tling was a feelings person, she thought. She realized that she thought of him as a person, as did the Wilsons, because he wore cord pants and tweed jackets. But he was an animal.

"I am animal," he remarked suddenly, reading her thoughts.

"So am I," said Ellen.

He smiled. His smile was instant, effortless,

like a child's. He hooked her arm in his on the way home.

"I can't talking with many people. Just — nothing to say. I want car. Go to countryside."

"I'll take you." Ellen worried; she was older than him.

"I no like young people," he added. "They really stupid." It turned out Tling was only twenty-five, but he thought of himself as older. "I am old," he said. "More old as you. Old as earth. Mine very old culture."

She listened to everything he said and she sympathized. "You understand me," said Tling to Ellen. "I think you know me very long time. *How* you know me?"

Rick and Rebecca Wilson invited Ellen and Tling to a New Year's party. They sat around a kitchen table making dumplings. You put a dab of meat mixture in the centre of a flat rolled circle of dough. Then you folded the edges together and squeezed along the rim to seal the join. The edge should look fluted, like the edge of a pie shell.

Everyone praised Ellen's handiwork with the dumplings. Tling gathered them and put them in a pot to boil. When he sat down he pressed his feet and his legs against hers under the counter. The Wilsons beamed.

While she drove him home, Tling held on to Ellen so tightly that she became not herself, but something about him. It was delicious, a transport. Men and apes had this in their power to give.

Tling's apartment was two small rooms over a store on Broadview, overlooking the Don Jail. He pushed her up against the wall. Their love-making was inspired. Exotic. Peaceful, at the end.

"Bodies, same every place," said Tling.

"Nearly," Ellen said. It was the coarse long hair that grew almost everywhere, its nap and crowns on the inside of his arms; it was the bare skin where you found it that seemed more naked than her own.

He stroked her breasts.

"Great apes and humans, ninety-nine percent same genetic makeup," he said and started again.

Later they lay on their sides; one in front, one tucked in behind. "Dumplings," Tling said.

"This is so strange. Who would have imagined it? Me from here and you from—"

God wrote it down on Ellen's exposed side. He leaned down with his long sharp finger and scratched slow deliberate characters on her back, the curve of her waist, over her hip, down the side of her thigh.

When she ran her hand over the welts she was pleased.

"Look," she said. "God is writing a novel."

"I know," said Tling. "It's about me."

Much later, Tling woke, sweating.

"Crisis," he cried. He had drunk too much. He got up and roamed his two small rooms, hitting the walls. "I lose everything," he raved. "My jungle, my tribe, my freedom—"

Ellen cried. "I am sorry for you," she said.

He stopped to embrace her.

"You give me something. You give me back feeling. Feeling very strong." Then he went back to raving and pacing. He would stay awake now until five in the morning and then go back to sleep most of the day. He was not yet on human time.

Throughout the next few days Ellen thought constantly of Tling. He was a grave animal, short in stature, with quantities of long silky grey hair almost everywhere. Only his hands and feet, his ears and the circle of his face were exempt. His nose was small and flat, his lips folded under, his eyes opaque and dark. His ears were enormous, like cupped hands. His big toes worked like thumbs, in opposition; making love, it was as if he had four hands. The dense serenity of his presence, the delicacy of his long thin wrinkled fingers, his sudden childish laugh, made him delightful to her.

They became lovers. Ellen realized early on he was going to be difficult. He had a well-developed sense of his own significance. As well, he was wary. Their political backgrounds were so different. Except the Wilsons, no one knew. Tling did not like parties. He refused to meet her friends. "I am animal," he said. "Don't like social. This we do—" he meant the love-making— "no one must know. If I go everyplace with you, people talk."

He justified the isolation for her sake.

"I come from far away. I am live here for short time only, then go back. You here long time. You woman. You must careful."

In the countryside, they drove from town to town. Tling loved the crumbling relics of rural life. A collapsing barn made him clap with pleasure. A brick farmhouse, abandoned in a rocky field, moved him so much he made her stop the car so he could get out and cry. In graveyards he ran from stone to stone, exclaiming over their shapes, asking Ellen to read. "Beloved wife of; beloved husband of..." It made him laugh to see the dead claimed. "Human very funny," he told Ellen. "Apes just go away, dead body." She taught him the word "sentimental."

When she came to pick him up he would be leaning over his tacky balcony looking into the parking lot. But when she arrived at his door, it would be ajar, with no sign of him. She had to search for him, behind the refrigerator, in the bathtub under a towel. When discovered, he launched himself into her arms. "This game I play with my mother," he would say.

He liked to frighten her. Tling might sob or laugh over lunch or break into shrill keening sobs. He might erupt in anger, twist his torso from the hips, allowing his arms to swing out, growl, show his teeth. Quickly she learned to enjoy the danger. It was a point of pride with Ellen that she could handle his temperament. Each fit was followed by affection and helplessness. "You magic!" he would murmur.

Tling developed a deathly fear of the strange woman who inhabited the lobby of his apartment building. She wore a turban and filthy brown robes. "Where she go?" he would ask when she disappeared into the stairwell.

"Nowhere. She's just hiding," said Ellen. "She comes back every night. She's homeless."

"She has no tribe, no people?"

"It happens," said Ellen.

Homeless became Tling's new word. "I too. I homeless. Have no home," he would say.

This was how he learned words, picking them up like bright stones. They dazzled him. "I'm a MAD— —man!" he announced one night, after he popped out from behind the shower curtain. This went with a growl and Tarzan stretch; he got it from television.

"I think I am monkey they put up in sky," he said one night. "You know famous monkey?"

"Now he's freeze-dried," said Ellen. She had seen that monkey in the Air and Space Museum in Washington. It seemed grotesque even then.

Ellen loved Tling. She adored his dainty feral odour, the fine silky hair, the tougher exposed skin. Staring into his eyes brought her to the edge of some memory, some mystery she could not name. He had a quality of stillness, of rest, which she had never known. She imagined his specific gravity was different; he was heavier than she, he occupied space more fully. The wonder of it was that despite the heaviness of his life, the fact that he was a prisoner here, a refugee, that he was freeze-dried, had no one, and nothing, that he had lost all his tribe and only music could travel with him (all those woes he rehearsed daily), he paid attention to her.

"Why you no marry? he said. "You very hard working? I think you need play, like me."

Ellen's friends and her father complained that she was neglecting them. One day when Ellen arrived at Tling's apartment for tea, she threw her purse in the corner, howled, and squeezed tears from her fisted eyes. She kicked a couple of doors. Well, he could do it.

"I hate families!" she said. "I hate looking after my father! I hate my friends! These people, they think they own me." Tling listened to her carefully and nodded. "Of course, of course," he said. "You right. Is terrible. You no free."

Tling paced that day. He rotated his trunk, swinging his arms out. "*Who* is refugee? *Who* is prisoner?" he announced rhetorically. "I no run from family. *You* run. In my jail, I is free. Free of life. *You* is prisoner."

Others of Tling's kind came to the city, some lucky others who had escaped the purges and the poachers. Mu, who wore thick glasses, stood back admiring Ellen, with one finger on his lips. Sinbad was different, an introvert. They went to Roy Thompson Hall to hear the Toronto Symphony. The three apes argued heatedly in their language for half an hour afterward about whether Mozart or Beethoven was number one.

"God gave me music and he gave me love," said Tling that night, "but he took away the rest." Unfortunately both music and love required great concentration, and tired Tling out. Often now when they came in at night he would not make love to Ellen. Instead he raged: he hated money, he did not want to work, he could not read or write and therefore could not join in society. Besides, he was an ape, and people did not accept him. He became lethargic. His face grew puffed with sleep and too much television.

One day Ellen left school at noon, appearing at his bedside with hands on her hips. "You must get outside," she said. "See people. Get exercise. Breathe fresh air. It's beautiful." It was a sunny day in March; spring was just under the surface.

"No," he screamed. "No outside. No beautiful!" He lay on the bed and kicked his feet.

Somehow the winter wore to its end.

In April, Tling and Ellen went to the zoo. It was very quiet there. And cold. The ground was bare, with little frozen puddles scattered like jewels in the dead grass. They walked from cage to cage. The heated monkey houses smelled, but Tling stood laughing and making faces. The monkeys ignored him. His closest relative there was a baboon, but he would not speak to Tling.

"Not same language," said Tling. "Ape classical. Baboons very low animals. No culture. Just like sex and eat."

He liked the Siberian tiger, so beautiful, so sad, padding from one corner of his enclosure to the other. "Like me," he said. "Just like me. Tiger depressed. In cage. No home, no family." He paced back and forth outside the cage. When they were leaving Tling said, "I think I like zoo. I come here, stay with other animals."

"I would miss you."

"You come too. We live in cage together. Let people stare."

Later, in bed, she lay on top of him. She asked him what he would like her to do, to please him.

"Male simple, easy to please. In sex male is just worker for the female," he says.

Ellen was frustrated. She didn't want him to be the worker. She wanted to catch him off guard.

"Your face is a mask," she said. "What happens if you take it off?" She pretended to lift the mask off his face. He jumped out of bed, raging.

"Never laugh at me! I come from far back, time. I you father. You father father. You father father father. If no me, then no you."

"Yes," she said, stroking the hair on his chest to calm him. "I'm sorry." She had forgotten about his pride. "Yours very old culture."

"I come here like baby, have nothing. Need help. But I am great ape," he said.

Ellen rented a cottage from a friend. It was a log cabin on a hilltop, overlooking a valley with a winding river. In the moonlight the drifts of snow beside the road shone like starched sheets. There were fences to climb, hills to roll down. Ellen thought Tling would go out and play in the snow but he wouldn't. He wanted to play house. He swept the floor. When Joni Mitchell's song about clouds came on the radio, Tling sang along. He had heard it when he was a baby at the jungle station. Ellen lay on her back and made angels in the snow. "You crazy," he said admiringly.

Together they cooked three meals a day—the coconut juice and vegetables and eggs he liked, and a little meat for her. The second day, drinking coffee at the kitchen table, they told the stories of their previous loves. Tling had been mated at seven to a young ape who was later killed by poachers. He fell in love with a white woman who worked at the jungle station.

"She was not beautiful," he said. But she was smart and knew a lot about apes. He wanted to go with her to California, where she lived, but she would not take him. She came to visit him every year. One year Tling found her ugly, and old. "I take new lover," he said categorically.

"Do apes usually have one lover for life?" said Ellen.

"I tell you this," he said. "Apes very funny. Yes, have wife. Almost all year, stay with wife, sleep with tails together, like this." Across the table, he wound his arm through and around hers. "Defend territory. Sit in trees, scream other apes go away. Then, sudden, one day, everybody crazy. Make love everybody else. Wife, husband, many lovers. Forget it, territory. Forget it, family. Then, okay, all over. Apes go home. Husband to wife. Wife to husband. Kiss, no more angry. Tails together go sleep. Raise family. But—" he said, raising his arms "—no *really* family. Really, somebody else baby. And your baby, some other family get. Still, protect family, protect territory. Again, until next season. Scientist think this very funny," he concluded. "But I like."

Ellen described how she had been married at twenty to a graduate student who never finished his degree. "Live off my money!" she exclaimed. She enlarged her story, a trick she had learned from Tling. Mother died, father *hates* every man she chooses. Once he chased her man off the porch with an upended chair. He says terrible things to them. So, she dated men who did not understand English—a Mexican, and then an Israeli. They don't mind his temper. But they don't marry her.

"Husband one thing. Lover another," said Tling. "Husband like horse, must work, must make life. Lover is like tiger, make big roar, then lie down. I am like tiger," said Tling.

Ellen searched out the ape references in the English literary canon. She found only Masefield's precious cargo of ivory, apes and peacocks; and in *The Taming of the Shrew*, the curious reference, "and, for your love to her, lead apes in Hell." Robert Browning had said "What's time? Leave now for dogs and apes! Man has forever!"

"Perhaps we've been unfair to the ape," mused Ellen. "Only God understands him."

Ellen felt the hard nib of His finger again, its cursive scratch along her spine.

"Nobody understand. Not even God." Tling began to cry. "Not good novel He writing."

"You are ridiculous," said Ellen to Tling.

He brightened up, with this new trinket. "I hear this word many time on TV. I think very

important word. What does it mean, ridiculous?"
said Tling.

In the beginning she had loved his lack of
words. It meant they could not argue. Now it meant
she could not make herself understood. His needs—
so great, so fetchingly dramatized—dominated
every moment. Even Ellen's dreams were taken
over by his dreams of jungle and pursuit. His pow-
erlessness became hers. In the beginning Tling appeared to offer her his attentions. But she had
slipped aside of that, she had let him take the light,
she had turned herself into his handmaiden. Ellen
knew she did this sort of thing with men. It was a
bad habit.

Ellen told Rick Wilson's committee that
Tling was having a difficult time adjusting to the
fact that he could not go back to Borneo.

The inevitabilities were falling into place. It is all
in the characters, you see. God has created Ellen in
such a way that she falls in love with a man for his
manifest destiny. She likes a star-crossed man, a
burdened man, a Prometheus caught in a web of giant forces. It does no good to ask why. Perhaps it
makes her feel powerful to provide insight and caring. She can struggle to unlock his trap, without
having to fear his unleashed strength. Then, too, a
man with enormous problems puts her in the shade;
even to herself, she becomes invisible.

Ellen began to push Tling. Go out and meet people. Write up a resumé. Get insurance. Let down your pride. Do some work. Help me, at least. But God had created Tling, too. He made him deaf to importunings, inert until enraged, overly proud. Because he could not change, Tling began to see Ellen as his enemy. She was like a German. She was hard; she had no more magic, only rules; she was not really crazy. She wanted a work horse, not a tiger.

Still, they loved.

"You are brave, very brave," he said. "But brave is not enough, for the life. And beside you are woman. Want family."

"I don't. If I wanted that I could find it," Ellen told him, though she didn't believe it. She imagined running away to live with him in Hawaii. They could teach an interdisciplinary course. Then she cried. She knew he couldn't be a husband.

"But I love you and so I want to," he said.

In May, Ellen went to a conference. The night she left, Tling threw a tantrum.

"Crisis!" he cried again. "I am like a tree, I go down," he said, brokenly. "I lose everything— lose freedom, lose life, lose country!" He rehearsed the impossible nature of his situation. "I can't go home. I can't live here. Not in city. I can't take job. Ape not for jobs." He peeked up from where he had his face pressed into the pillow. "I think I go to die," he said.

Ellen lay beside him, listening. "Do you

think you are angry because I am going away?" she said, finally.

"Maybe a little," he said, cheerfully.

On her trip she longed for Tling. She imagined him hiding behind the doors at her meetings, floating on his back with his hands behind his head in the hotel swimming pool. When she arrived home she telephoned. He was going to the Wilsons the next night and she must come. She offered to pick him up but he said no.

Tling looked wonderful. His face was clear, the skin taut and alive. He stood formally in his blue blazer, his hands with their delicate long hair on the backs crossed in front of his genitals, in the self-protecting way of men. He flashed his rictus smile, lips up over teeth. With him was a woman with a Celtic look, red-haired and wiry.

"I meet Marilou at conference on animal rights. Marilou is help me. Teach me to write, read letters."

Ellen's heart plunged desperately and then set up a threatening march pace. She spoke to Marilou; her face flamed.

Tling too was acting oddly. Since their first mad week he had allowed himself no single possessive touch or look in public. But today he pressed her thigh, squeezed her hand half unseen, and winked his powerful black eye, until finally, pleading jet lag, she backed out the door.

"Marilou say me *who* is that pretty woman," Tling said the next day on the telephone. "You always pretty but yesterday party you *too* pretty. Do you find new lover?"

"I don't," Ellen cried indignantly. "Why would I?" (*Where would I?* was what she was saying to herself.) There were certain advantages to Tling's not being human. He did not know, for instance, how difficult it was to find men in academe. Whereas Tling was male, he was probably even endangered. He would easily find new women.

Sitting in the campus coffee shop she read a "Multitudes" poster. "A Parliament of owls, a Shrewdness of apes." Yes, Tling was shrewd. He had fooled her.

God's penpoint went wild. Ellen's skin rose up like hives.

"We must talk," she said to his message machine.

When she entered the tiny apartment, Tling was hiding. She looked dispiritedly in the closet, behind the refrigerator, in the shower and behind the curtains. The curtains she had donated after a neighbour complained of Tling in the window, fully illuminated and unclothed. Nude was what she said, but it didn't apply, said Ellen, with all that hair.

Finally she sat on the sofa bed and said, "I give up."

Tling threw himself at her, embracing her knees.

"I am bad animal. I tell you true because you special, so smart, give me warm. I do find new lover."

Ellen stood up stiffly. His arms slid down to her ankles.

"I try to explain you. Always same. Take lover for two three month, then—new lover."

"Why?"

"No reason. Just for new. Season change."

"I can't believe you did it. You broke it," she says.

"You broke it first."

"I did not!" cries Ellen. "It was so good." She pounded his back.

Tling was still holding on to her knees.

"You don't love me? You're crazy. You do love me. You must love me. It was good, it was so good."

Sobbing and shouting at the same time, Ellen fell to the floor on top of Tling. It was possible to be sincere, but also enjoy the performance. Tling crawled out from under her. He lay on the floor weeping. His voice was high and shrill. Tears fell from his eyes onto her insteps.

"You need husband. For life, horse. I am only for lover. Short time."

Ellen was insulted. "I don't need a husband."

Tling cried. "You very kind me. Friend. So good friend."

"I'm not your friend. I won't be your friend."

"Friend higher as lover," explained Tling. "Friend number one."

She did not care if friend was number one.

Ellen took a sick day and went back to the cabin. She played sad music and made herself cry. She danced around the cabin, laughing at Tling's dirty jokes, groaning at his laziness, his tantrums, his self-ishness. She ground her teeth and pledged that she would get over it. She mourned his touch, his crude jokes, his soft hair. Three days later she drove home, purged and clean and finished with Tling.

But it wasn't finished.

They went for long walks together.

"*Why* did you end it? It was so good," cried Ellen.

"No reason. No why," said Tling. "I am stupid. Just— ridiculous."

They cried and shook their fists at each other. Ellen threw tantrums herself. He threw them back. Tling continued to see Marilou. Ellen became Tling's friend. He found a job, and a new apartment. He finished with Marilou and found another woman, but Ellen didn't know her name.

Endings are so difficult, thinks God. The story must stop, must have a reason to stop, but not end, because for God, there is no end.

One day, Ellen woke up and decided that Tling was right. She should find a man, a nice safe workhorse, and marry him. And she did. It so happened her man was blind. He liked to run his fingers over the welts which covered her body, God's script, in braille. Sometimes she jumped out of bed, and yelled "Crisis!" For an hour or more she screamed, and roamed around the house hitting walls. When she was finished she fell at his feet and kissed his ankle bones. The blind man was a good listener.

"Why?" said Ellen.

"Because," said Tling. They were walking along the boardwalk in the Beaches where they went, every few weeks, together. Tling was a success story, a fund raiser for the Wilderness Society, a heart breaker who rubbed the bottoms of women's feet and made them swoon, asked them to be his mother, and then threatened to kill himself.

Ellen was written all over; her stomach, the insides of her arms and legs, every available inch of exposed skin inscribed. She is still being written on, a postscript here and there.

"Because," said Tling. "*I* ridiculous. "*You* ridiculous. Love ridiculous. Because the life, you know, is ridiculous."

The Psychic
Renovators

"Toward the end decade of the twentieth century," wrote Roger Boynton, "Toronto housing stock was taken over by successive waves of settlers. These settlers acquired what was known as 'real estate' for the security of their families and as its principal expression of wealth. Such permanence proved illusory, however; each decade previous inhabitants moved on, and new families took over."

He admired his careful script. Roger intended to place this record of his accumulated wisdom in a time capsule. A group he belonged to, calling itself the Centre for Planetary Wisdom, had asked him to contribute. The time capsule, which would also contain batting averages of major-league ball players, the video "Roger Rabbit," and a copy of the defeated Meech Lake Accord, as well as a collection of restaurant menus, was to be buried at the intersection of Yonge and St. Clair. The members also hoped to have a duplicate time capsule dropped off on Mars by the American space program. Without being self-important, one had to preserve a sense of one's own significance in the grand scheme of things.

"The author's investigation in the municipal archives reveals a common practice of insuring real estate properties against theft and misadventure, save and except for what was called 'Acts of God.' Why floods, earthquakes and storms were considered Acts of God is unclear, especially since by this time less than 22 percent of Toronto-dwellers attended church."

Here Roger Boynton came to his favourite part.

"But houses proved difficult investments to protect. As well as Acts of God, denizens of the city had to contend with the profits and losses of the stock market, global trade realignment, and frequent marital splits and regroupings. These violent shifts had, among their more obvious affects, a way of easing houses prematurely onto the market. It was a strange fact too that properties thus hastened into sale had an enhanced allure to certain purchasers."

"These *psychic renovators*,'" he wrote, underlining the last two words with the flat tip of his calligraphy pen in Mediterranean-coloured ink from his fifty-dollar bottle, "were ambiguous figures. They were of course motivated by greed, seeking to profit from the distress of their fellow citizens. However, at the same time they were redemptive figures, attempting to reclaim homes for the traditional and spiritual values that still lurked in the walls."

He was proud of this coinage, 'psychic renovators.' "Values" and "lurked" he wasn't so sure of:
could a value lurk? If it didn't lurk, what did it do?
He didn't want to rewrite the whole paragraph just
to replace lurk with linger. It was his memory of the
renovators' type that urged him onward in his project. The Ethiers were his first. Their image came to
his mind still, and with startling clarity.

Laura and Howard Ethier stood side by side, he
with one hand gripping a briefcase, she with her
arms folded across her chest, before 18 Rusholme
Road. Their pose, to Roger, was reminiscent of
Grant Wood's 1930 painting "American Gothic." A
man and woman, a house, a landscape. But here
were no grim-faced homesteaders leading with
pitchfork into battle against untilled fields. Instead,
a lawyerish receded man in a navy blue suit and a
well-kept, leggy woman faced off against unim-
proved housing stock.

"Well, it's interesting," said Laura.

"Got charm," grunted Howard. Then silence.

"Owner's out of the country," said Roger.
He drove the spikes of a green and white For Sale
sign into the clover that was undermining the front
lawn.

"What's the situation?"

"He's seventy. Wife died. Something odd
about the family. He's estranged from his children,
or they won't help him, and he can't manage the
place. Spends a lot of time in Florida."

"Bargoon," said Laura and caught Howard's eye.

Laura Ethier was a tall, stooped woman, the sort men like to say are over-educated and underemployed. Ten years before, when Laura was first married, Roger had showed her a house on Madison that had been forced into sale because the owner had not complied with city orders to bring the plumbing and wiring up to standard. It was a speed house; the door opened and creatures scuttled for the corners, but they weren't cockroaches, they were human beings. Laura held her nose and put in an offer for fifty thousand. On closing day the speed freaks vanished, leaving only their bundled blue jeans and ragged blankets, and a few curling issues of *Rolling Stone*.

Laura gutted the house herself, opening up all the walls and staircases. Head in a kerchief, her smock coated with grey dust, she swung her hammer and dragged out long sheets of plastic loaded with collapsed plaster. She put up wallboard and painted it all white, which was the fashion.

When it was done, she and Howard moved in. Their first child was born at home, under the care of a midwife, in an open-concept nursery that overlooked the living room. While expecting her second Laura remembered the attractions of rooms, with noise-absorbing walls and doors that closed. That time Roger found them a three-story semi on Bellefair in the Beaches. Again it was a good buy, a bankruptcy. The owners had opened a restaurant on Queen when interest rates were eighteen percent, borrowing against their home.

Babies in carriage and playpen, Laura spent two years redoing Bellefair. She put decks front and back, a porthole window and skylights in the third floor, laminated kitchen cupboards. When Roger dropped by to visit she was standing on a stepladder, roller painting the kitchen ceiling. While she rollered, she talked to the children. The house had been unloved. No meals had been cooked there, no bedtime stories read by the fire.

"We'll change all that, won't we?" she repeated. The babies rolled on their backs to watch.

Now the Ethiers surveyed the outside of 18 Rusholme, looking into the downspouts, poking at cracks in the brick and squinting up to see the angle of sunlight over the trees. It was a huge house, square, a mildly individualized version of a type built in the better parts of Toronto in the 1920's— mock Tudor, with black beams striping the white facing under two peaks, a side gable, a wide, covered porch. It stood on the corner of Rusholme and Dewson where— for a few blocks only—the houses were set on generous lots, as if a spate of affluence had caused the builders to reconsider, however temporarily, the usual mean semis hunkered down on the pavement. But its grace was diminished by an air of inwardness. A row of tall spruce trees hid the lower part of the house from view, and vines covered the second-story windows.

"Want to go in?" said Roger.

"Not yet."

Roger Boynton's card cited his membership

in the Gold Circle, meaning he'd sold over two million dollars in real estate in the past year. Often he accomplished a sale by behaving exactly as he did now, brushing the dust off a windowsill as if uncertain whether he ought to even try to persuade. He knew better than to rush. He occupied the long, boring stretches of time while his clients deliberated by observing, and had thus become a student of marital politics.

Roger was divorced. He and his wife and child went for family counselling around the time he was admitted to the Gold Circle. His wife complained that he was never home, that he paid no attention to their son. By way of making conversation the counsellor asked the boy, who was seven, what he wanted to be when he grew up. The boy said he wanted to be a client.

"You see!" Roger's wife crowed bitterly. "That's all he ever hears: 'I'm going to see a client,' 'I've got to phone a client.' No wonder they're his heroes." Later, she added, "I'm convinced Roger would sell his own mother if someone offered cash."

That hit Roger hard. In fact, his mother would have been as likely to sell him. She dealt in collectibles and antiques. Family legend had it she sold the crib he was sleeping in before his first birthday. To his mother, resale was rebirth. Selling was shedding age. Buying, on the other hand, was an expression of hope, of the belief in improvement, a renegotiation of conditions. Roger knew instinctively what the buyer was thinking: in this ideal setting I shall at last be permitted to live my ideal life.

In a few minutes he unlocked the front door. The Ethiers stood in the beaded pattern of light that fell on the parquet floor of the entrance hall.

"Great leaded glass," he said.

Howard stood back narrow-eyed, trying to get the whole picture, while Laura poked the intricately carved lamps on the newel posts, eyed the oak ceiling beams and the central staircase that went around at right angles.

Eventually, Laura and Howard drifted back toward the front door.

"Definite potential," said Laura, biting her lip so as not to betray her excitement. "Fireplaces. Window seats." She let her hand rest on a brass doorknob as she eyed the leaded glass doors on the dining room cabinets. "Built ins. Did his wife die or what?"

"The first one, yeah." Roger paused. "The owner is a guy called Angus Otis. Retired labour leader, I gather. He and his wife raised their family here. She died, and then—well," Roger attempted an offhand laugh. "The way they tell it, his second wife murdered his third."

Laura ran her hand over the wood of the built in cabinets in the dining room. "Oh my goodness," she said. "I love it." It was unclear whether she meant the story or the house.

"Oh, here we go," said Howard unhappily.

Howard was only dimly aware of what animated his wife. He found it easier that way. A shorter, thicker, altogether more quiescent person than Laura, Howard was a downtown lawyer with a bulky, short body and eyes that blinked. In the seventies he didn't demonstrate, but instead served as a legal adviser to students who occupied the U.S. Consulate. When he met Laura, the protestor, he stuck to her: changing women would have hurt. Laura was meant to deflect the future for him, and failing that, to interpret it.

Howard said he didn't have much time and kept edging back to the door.

"Roger, thanks for showing it to us," said Howard.

"Be in touch, eh?"

Now the agent left them alone. Laura wanted the house; Howard was holding back. Roger knew better than anyone what would happen next. He'd seen it before, their dance to reach mutual assent. First, Laura would lobby. She would tell Howard she needed a new house to work on, something more to do. She would remark on how easy it would be to sell Bellefair at a profit because she'd done it over so beautifully. As long as she worked on him Howard would resist. Then, suddenly, Laura would appear to give up. "I'm tired of trying to talk you into what's best for you," she would say, and abruptly cease to speak of the house on Rusholme.

Poor Howard. His own stubbornness hooked him. He couldn't forget the house. By the end of two weeks the very idea he fought would have taken root, though he would give no sign of a change of heart.

A week later Howard re-opened the subject.

"You know, the Beaches has got so horribly trendy. It's downright offensive," he complained one night when they were out on Queen Street for a drink. "Did you read that piece about the teenage gangs around here? That's probably one of them now." They walked past a couple of kids writing with felt marker on a bus shelter. "Whatever happened to that house on Rusholme?"

Finding the history on a house was Howard's job. He enjoyed nothing so much as a good title search. He had searched the title of their Madison house, and the Bellefair one too. He was used to the dry pages, the long typescript of names and addresses and dates. Title records presented events by transaction, a version of life over which, by virtue of his legal training, he had mastery. This time, down at City Hall, in the little cubicle with the documents for 18 Rusholme, he found very little. The house had been owned by Angus Otis for thirty years, and before that by the family who built it. But Howard recalled the story of the murder, and sent a student over to get newspaper files on the story.

"Got yourself a good one," the student said, plunking the copies on Howard's desk. There, gripped, Howard read how Angus and Mary Otis had been happily married for twenty-one years, but then she had died, and Otis began to run with a "fast group of widowers and divorcees from Mississauga," as the *Sun* put it. He met and married someone called Flora, but within a short time the marriage was annulled.

After the annullment, Angus married a third time, this time a woman called Rosemary Custer. But Angus and Flora were not finished with each other, or so said Angus's lawyers. Flora was distraught. She telephoned him at work, waylaid him at lunch and drove past his home in the dark. Finally one day she went to the house on Rusholme Road and stabbed Rosemary in the back eleven times with a knife she had hidden in her skirt.

Finally Howard sat back and rubbed his eyes. He had been staring at pages of type all day. He went home to tell Laura. "The case kept being delayed. Took two years. Flora pleaded not guilty by reason of self defence, but that didn't wash because of the stabs in the back. She went to jail for life but after a couple of years the feminists got her out. Said she was suffering too much in jail, losing weight. She had 'failure to thrive.'"

"Just like a baby." Laura's voice was hushed.

"So Flora must be walking the streets now, a free woman."

"Roger said this 'Angus' guy's kids wouldn't talk to him. No wonder. And he wants to sell so they won't get the house because he figures they don't deserve it."

"You talk about houses having vibes." Howard leaned over the coffee table. He put one elbow down, opened his mouth in a distorted yawn and, using his two forefingers and his thumbs, deftly popped out first one contact lens and then the other. He was like a man who had crossed the highway and had a good look at a messy accident and now wanted to get away. "You want to watch out with this house. You go in there and start renovating you let loose all those—I don't know, ions, or something, that have been glued in with the wallpaper..." he said. He didn't finish his sentence.

Laura wasn't listening anyway. "That a family could descend to that, erupt in that! This normal married man and wife and their kids!" She thought of her own little brood—the kids now twelve and ten. It was dreadful to contemplate what this world could deliver. You had to put your foot down somewhere. You had to fight for innocence. "And the house had so much potential," she mused. Its accoutrements were of a particular kind: breakfast nook, window seats, laundry chute, front porch; the backyard nicely flat for croquet, the stoned area perfect for barbecues. Their contemplation drew Laura into nostalgia for family life before the fall in the fifties. They'd get a dog. The screen door would slam on summer nights. Kids would put up lemonade stands on the curb.

"Don't be ridiculous, there are no *ions* in the wallpaper. And if there were you'd just scrub them out," she said, snappishly. She hated getting excited about something she couldn't have. And she refused to wheedle with Howard. "What a creepy story!" She settled down in front of the television, determined not to think about Angus and Flora and poor Rosemary.

Howard called Roger and said they wanted to look at the house again. When they arrived, Angus was there. He was short and stocky with a bulldog's stance. His silver hair made him seem more distinguished than perhaps he was. He was definite and firm in every word he uttered. Here was how to turn off the hot-water heater, this was the garage door opener, the water filter; the window screens went on the twenty-fourth of May weekend—no earlier, no later. He strode across the backyard to point out the tangle of black raspberry canes.

"They only bear every second year, but they're excellent. My wife used to make pies."

Which wife? Laura asked silently. She made delighted noises but she pledged, if they bought, to pull out the canes right away. Raspberry pies would be nice, but only after Angus was exorcised.

In the basement, Angus showed Howard his tools.

"I'll just leave this all here. I have no use for any of it now."

Even Howard was stirred, looking at the workbench. All the hammers, pliers, wrenches, wire suspended from s-hooks on a frame. All the screws of different sizes in plastic boxes. So ordered, and each with a purpose. The workbench made one believe that it was possible to fix anything that went wrong. Just before he shut the workroom door, Angus picked up a heavy red axe that stood in the corner.

"And this," he said to Howard, winking, "is to make Laura dance."

That night, Laura sobbed.

"You never said anything to him. You never said one thing. You let him stand there, and practically threaten to kill me—"

"It was a joke, with the axe."

But even Howard didn't think it was much of a joke. "Come on, Laura," he said, hugging her, "*he*'s not the murderer of the piece. The murderer was Flora."

"Now I see why they got her out of jail. He mesmerized that poor woman until she committed the murder he wanted her to."

"I've never heard anything so ridiculous in my entire life," said Howard. "When we buy this house we're going to have to forget about Angus and Flora."

"Oh Howard," said Laura, "I knew you would." She threw her long arms around his neck.

On closing day Angus appeared with Roger to hand over the keys. He had promised to empty the basement, but made only a half-hearted attempt, leaving behind a great many soggy mattresses and boxes of musty books and half-empty jars of household cleaner and bales of wire and broken mops. Normally Laura would have refused to close, but she just wanted the old man out of there, so she said nothing. He had a certain creepy magnetism that made her want to deal with him briskly He held an orange plastic cup with a lid, and SPILL AND SPELL on it in black. The cup was full of keys. It was an oddity of the house that each room had its own lock.

Angus handed over the cup. "I want you to know that selling this house is the most traumatic thing that has ever happened to me."

You mean more traumatic having your second wife murder your third? thought Laura. But Angus's undefeated blue-eyed look defied contradiction. Laura could only ask herself why, if they were such a close family, all those locks?

The locks were the first thing Laura went after. She got Howard to take a jigsaw and cut them out of all the doors. She had nightmares that the children locked themselves in a room and she was desperately fingering her way through the orange plastic cup but no key would free them. Once the locks were gone there were these awful, jagged, fist-sized holes in the maple. The handyman cut matching odd-shaped wooden plugs to fill the holes, which he then patched with plastic wood, and stained to match the varnish. Still the patching showed.

During the subsequent renovations, Laura did try to forget Angus Otis, but the old man mocked her from every corner: painted nudes on basement walls, sinks tucked inside corner cupboards, a wooden shingle reading "fishermen make better lovers," an old shotgun, a corkscrew with a wooden handle in the shape of a little boy peeing. Every time she cleaned out a drawer she wondered which wife had left the plastic liner. An apron with an embroidered F, discovered under the bathroom pipes, made her scream. And there was an awful coffee mug with the name "Angus" on it, which Howard insisted on keeping.

The axe, by this time, had become a family joke. They all spoke about "burying the hatchet," but in fact they kept it, just where Howard had left it, in the basement. Laura herself dined out on the story, to the point where its power seemed to have gone away. She had to live with the axe. She no longer had the energy to move on.

Years passed, and Roger Boynton visited again. He thought he might interest Laura in another property.

The fir hedge was short and thick now, the ivy cut down and the yard surrounded by a row of neat pickets. Laura had had the porch roof replaced with a recessed skylight and put out some potted plants and Muskoka chairs.

"It's a wonderful place to sit," said Laura. "But I rarely sit there, or anywhere," she said.

Roger found Laura changed. She seemed not to remember the dream of Arcadian family life that had attached to this house. A restlessness had seized her. Howard was working longer hours, the children were away at baseball and ballet. In spring and summer she worked in the garden. She'd done a good job on Rusholme Road but he could see it would never show well, and they'd have trouble getting their money out in what was now a falling market.

"Get thee behind me," she said to Roger.

"I'll never do another. I wish I hadn't even tackled this one."

"What about Howard?" said Roger.

"Now that the house is done Howard's very pleased. He's completely forgotten his resistance. No ions interfere with his peace. Howard's lucky that way," said Laura.

So endeth the career of a psychic renovator, Roger thought. He had only visited the Ethiers one more time. And that was under unusual circumstances. He'd got a call: old Angus Otis's son wanting to see the old place: would Roger introduce him to the owners?

When they pulled up at the kerb, Laura was in the garden. Roger could see that Laura had no idea who it was; this middle-aged, sandy-haired man in green pants and a white shirt rolled up at the elbows. The woman who got out of the car after him was short with a neat khaki skirt belted at the waist and a pink golf shirt with a little green man on a horse, swinging a club right over her left breast where her heart ought to be. She looked equally innocuous, but as they confronted Laura she began to have a strange feeling. It was as if they wanted something, as if they were a delegation.

Then she saw Roger.

"Visitors," he said. "From the past."

The younger man held out his hand. "Frank Otis," he said.

"You're kidding," said Laura. She gave him a severe look. Laura had become harder, more herself with age: now she looked straight at the man and said, "I always wondered what became of the sons of fathers who ran with fast crowds of widowers and whose serial wives began murdering each other."

There was a hush. But Frank Otis was the soul of diplomacy, his chubby, slightly shining face untroubled as it sought Laura's approval. He looked like homogenized milk. He had short hair and horn-rimmed glasses, he could pass for anyone.

"This is what becomes of them," he said, and handed Laura a card. It read:

FRANK OTIS
FAMILY COUNSELLING—
DIVORCE NEGOTIATION
MEDITATION—MEDIATION

She laughed and laughed, just like her old self. As if something had been set free inside her.

"Well I think we have something in common," she said. "I've been living with your father all this time, undoing his work. I guess you have too."

The last person to get out of the car was a girl of about twelve, with dirty blonde hair and pink shorts, and a T-shirt with rainbows dotted all over it.

"My daughter, Rebecca," said Frank.

Rebecca didn't look anyone in the eye and she wasn't interested in what they'd done to the house. She stood with her hair hanging in front of her face, making her presence felt by emitting an intense need. Frank's wife, who had been introduced as Diane, stood attentively by, smiling and nodding when Frank glanced at her for confirmation. The talk flowed over and around the thin obdurate figure of the girl until it became awkward to do anything except whatever it was she wanted.

"My daughter wanted to look for something her grandpa left for her in the basement."

"What was it exactly?" Laura did not want to say that all there was left of Angus in this basement was the axe.

"It was a little bag of gold coins. She says Dad put it in there, under the floor. She never forgot. Talked about it for years."

"Go ahead please," said Laura, leading her to the door. They all followed. Frank looked in the direction of his daughter's back, preparing a hearty response no doubt, for when she came back without it. "I was angry with my father for years, and kept her away from him. Now that he's dead I kinda wish I'd let her come."

Laura was annoyed to find she suddenly felt at fault, as if it were she who had wounded this child, she who had deprived her of treasures to be returned to.

"It must have disappeared with the workmen—believe me, our children never went near that room. They think it's creepy." It came out of her mouth a little more aggressively than she intended.

They waited for Rebecca. Laura fingered Frank's business card. Roger Boynton shifted his feet and looked at the floor and wondered if there were any way, any way at all he was going to get a listing or a new client out of this.

Then Rebecca opened the door from the cellar.

"Was it there, honey?"

You still couldn't see the child's face for hair.

"No."

"Not there?" said her mother in a voice slick with caring. They were the only two words she'd uttered thus far.

"No," said Rebecca.

"Oh, I'm sorry," said Laura, looking helplessly at Roger. "Really, it's been so long. And who'd have thought," she said to Roger, "there was anybody's treasure in all that mess down there."

"It's all right," said Rebecca tonelessly.

But it was not all right and Laura was bothered by it all that night and the next day.

The Orange Kite

When Ben looked out the window that morning in August the grey clouds were being hustled off the horizon by a quick west wind. The sky was finally blue. It was the last week of holidays; September, and school, which short weeks ago had been so far away you couldn't even glimpse it with binoculars, loomed on the horizon.

"Let's go for a picnic. Just one last one," he pleaded.

Nicola chimed in. "Let's go, let's go," she said. Ben usually hated it when his little sister agreed with him, but today he wanted her support. Nan looked at Charles; Charles looked at Nan. It didn't take much to persuade them.

"What will it be then, cookout, or sandwiches?" asked Nan, starting to move already. By this point in the summer she could organize a picnic in her sleep. They decided on hot dogs. Nicola wanted to be in charge of the fire, since she'd learned the teepee start at camp.

Nan dug out hotdogs and buns, Ben rounded up the dog Max, Nicola got the towels and Charles studied the maps. The Pancakes had a dock and fireplace but they'd been there once already this year. The sheltered islands behind their place were too easy for a day like today. It was a day to go out in the open.

"I'd like to go some place we've never been before," said Nan. "Let's go 'way out."

"We could try the Umbrellas," said Charles, looking at the sky. The Umbrellas were a long way out in open water, just a few specks on the map. "Trouble is if we hit a rock or the motor conks out, we'll be stranded."

"Maybe Brad and Marion can come," said Ben. He ran to the screen porch and looked over at the next island. Their neighbours' black boat was at the dock. Ben stood staring at the black boat. He wasn't sure about Brad any more.

"They're up," Nan said to Charles. "Want to ask them? We haven't seen them for ages."

"If we're going that far out it would be good to have two boats," said Charles.

"Let's ask them, let's ask them!" said Nicola.

Brad and Marion were adults, but they were as much the children's friends as their parents'. Brad used to teach Ben woodworking; he even tried to interest the boy in birds, but Ben preferred a game of cribbage. Brad had good luck finding the big pike, too. Marion was not his wife, but his friend, and she made good spaghetti. But it had been a bad couple of years for Brad and Marion.

They'd hardly been at their cottage at all, and when Ben and Nicola went over to visit, Brad would be busy or tired, and they'd have to go home soon.

"How come they hardly ever come here?" Ben asked his mother.

"Maybe the place is just too sad for them," said Nan.

"But isn't the sadness over yet?" said Ben. Still he gazed. He knew the reason for the trouble, because he'd been told. Brad's daughter had been killed in a car accident.

"Certain types of sadness go on for a long time. Sometimes they never go away."

"Never?"

"Maybe they change."

"Let's ask them," said Nicola, a girl of action.

Ben ran up the dock to call Brad on the party line. It was always busy when he called, because they shared a line. But he knew to hang up, and wait until the phone rang back at you. When he picked it up, Marion was on the line. She said she had some potato salad all made and they could be ready right away.

When his Dad pulled up at Brad's dock, Ben jumped out to tie up. It was his job now, and he was good at it. Brad and Marion's black boat was packed for the picnic. The men talked over the route while Marion hugged Nicola. Ben was about to push the boat away but at the last minute Brad jumped out and ran back up the path to the cottage. They all watched him.

Brad was stoop-shouldered and thin, his knees as sharp as a kid's. He loped unevenly up the path, the backside of his khaki shorts drooping, his T-shirt untucked from his waist. His longish black hair flew out from his scalp in wisps and his skin was pale and freckled, burning skin.

"What did he forget?" Ben said.

"Oh, it must be his toys," said Marion, smiling. She brushed her greying brown hair back into a ponytail and stuck it through the hole in the back of a baseball cap. The laugh lines were white around her eyes and mouth; her voice carried a touch of her Quebec origins.

He came out with a green garbage bag clutched in the middle with several sticks coming out the end.

"The kites," he said, gruffly.

"Do you want to ride with us, Nicola?" said Marion.

Looking over the back of his father's boat, Ben could see the smaller black boat in their wake, Nicola's bright orange life jacket like a buoy, Brad at the wheel in his yachting cap. Nan spread the map on her knees. The water was calm and flat, heaving here and there as if with breath, giving no hint of its dangerous moods. They pointed straight out and drove and drove and drove; it seemed like an hour.

"Why do they call them the Umbrellas?" he asked his mother. She showed him on the map: there were eight islands, and they were clustered together in a curve with one large one at the centre, going lengthwise: it looked like an umbrella.

The islands materialized like a flotilla, islands made of magnificent grey-white rocks, worn to smooth humps like risen buns by the hammering waves. The granite was laced with bright orange lichen; in the crevices were tiny blue flowers and ferns.

They pulled up in their boat, slowly, on the lookout for shoals. When his father turned off the motor and drew up close to the edge of the rock shore, Ben jumped off the bow with the rope in his hands; as the boat glided in, he pushed it back out so it wouldn't bump. Nan climbed off the boat through the open front window. Charles handed down basket after basket, the bag with the bathing suits, and finally, Max, squirming and barking.

Brad and Marion landed. Nicola insisted that if Ben got to do the push off, she could throw the anchor off the back. But it was too heavy for her. Marion helped her, while Brad jumped down with his bag of kites in his hand.

"There's other people here!" said Ben. It seemed a betrayal.

"Where?"

"I can see brown on that island." The moving brown spot was on the next parabola rising from the glassy plane of the Bay.

"That's a dog."

Max spotted it and began to bark.

"It's people. I can see their boat."

"I don't mind seeing other people here," said Nan. "It's big enough. And anyway you never know when you're going to need help."

The children were in charge of choosing the firepit, and starting the fire. The adults walked all around "their" island. In the sunken centre where earth had collected, pine and red cedar grew, and raspberry and blueberry bushes. Nan and Marion began exclaiming over the moss and the berries, the colours of the rocks, the size of the pinecones, the depth of the water. It was the most beautiful blue green.

"I have to go in," said Nan.

She dove, and came up screaming. It was the kind of cold that made your bones ache. But she swam all the way around the island they'd landed on, getting out where she'd got in. It was a policy with Nan. Marion put in her toes and changed her mind. Then Max swam over to the next island to meet the other dog, and didn't know how to get back. He sat on a rock and barked until Nan swam across and pushed him into the water, and swam home again with him.

Silent as usual, Brad had already started to bring out his kites. The box kite, bright pink and green, had extra triangular flaps on its sides. He gave the bobbin to Nicola to hold.

"Maybe there's not enough wind," he said. But the box kite nearly leapt out of his hands and into the air. It tugged and pulled at his hands, rising straight upward until it was high, and steady.

"Hmm! More wind than I thought," he said. He chose another, a simple diamond shape, red and white, which sailed quickly upward. "Let's try this one," he said, pulling an orange kite with wide, bat-like wings and ferocious, oriental eyes with great black eyebrows painted on it.

"Okay," said Ben without enthusiasm. He didn't like the look of the orange kite: it was faded and the face on it was mean-looking. "I think that one is a bit old," he said, politely.

Brad went ahead and held it overhead. Ben pulled on the string. But the orange kite didn't fly. Brad was stubborn though. Finally, by pulling on the cord, and then letting it go into the wind he managed to get it up in the air straight over them. It dove and fluttered, in trouble, and then came down on its end, bouncing off the rock.

"That wind is deceptive," said Charles. They chose a protected spot to eat, where the smoke from their fire circled away from them. Brad hooked the kite bobbins under rocks and they flew overhead, like birds or guardian spirits, as they all sat down to roast their weiners. Every few minutes someone tugged on the strings, but the box kite and the red diamond needed no encouragement. They flew as high and as steadily as if they were hooked up somewhere in the heavens. Ben jumped and ran around the rocks as he ate.

"I can see the other boat," he said, with his mouth full of hotdog. "And the people can see us." He thought it looked as if there were two small boys there, but it was far enough away that he couldn't really tell if they were boys or girls. Ben hoped it was boys.

When the last beer was drained, Marion passed a bag of her chocolate chip cookies. The sun was high, and the adults lay languidly on the hot rocks under their flying flags, which had the huge open sky all to themselves. But two kites in the air wasn't enough for Brad; the orange one sitting on the rock seemed to bother him. He tried again, running with it, and got it flying.

"The wind is rising," said Brad, as the orange kite pulled steadily away from him.

Nan worried a little, being out in the open with rising wind. It felt cool at her back when she stood up from the sheltered place where they'd eaten. If it got too rough they'd have trouble getting back.

"I think the wind is rising," said Charles, looking over his shoulder to the southwest. On the exposed side of the island he could see little whitecaps on the water.

"Good for the kites, though." Brad gave the bobbin of the orange one to Ben, and went to get his fourth and last kite, a bigger box. It went up with no trouble at all. The four of them hung there in the air over the picnic island. Underneath, the picnickers felt very smug on their rock. A seagull went by to investigate the orange one, which looked like a bird.

"What is that supposed to be, a bat?" said Nicola.

"It's an old kite," said Marion, when Brad busied himself with the reel and didn't answer.

"It was Becky's kite, wasn't it Brad?" asked Ben. Ben always knew things before other people did.

"Hyup," said Brad. "I bought it for her when she was—well, maybe Ben's age. Only paid about a dollar for it."

Everyone was quiet for a minute and didn't know what to say. Brad didn't ever talk about his daughter. In fact, he hadn't even told them that she had died. It was only Marion who talked about it. Sometimes Nan asked Marion if they minded the kids going over so much, because she worried about it being painful for Brad. But Marion said no, they didn't mind, that it was good for him. "He's got to know that life goes on."

"That's the first time you ever said Becky to me," said Nicola, who would say anything.

Brad got very busy with his kites again.

Nan produced the coffee.

"What a luxury," Marion said. "Coffee on a picnic."

They'd eaten the cookies and the cherries; the hot-dog fire was reduced to low, grey ashes. When she drained her coffee cup Nan took the old yoghurt container she'd brought and went to pick raspberries.

Ben was turning himself around in circles, shifting the bobbin of the orange kite from hand to hand.

"They're leaving!" he announced.

The other boat pulled away from its sheltered anchor and set off to the north east, in the direction the wind was blowing. They all watched the boat as it left. Then they were alone on these rocks, the west wind at their backs, coming from hundreds of miles across the bay, across Lake Huron, from Michigan.

"Last chance for a rescue!" Nan said. "If

the boats don't start we're stuck here!"

"You always say things like that," said Nicola.

Ben, Nicola, Brad and Marion each had a kite in hand. "I've got five hundred feet of line on this one and it's all out," said Brad about the pink and green box kite. He began to reel in.

"There's a thousand on that orange one too, isn't there?" said Marion. After its slow start the orange kite was flying higher than any of the others. Ben held the reel loosely in his fingers and it just spun itself out and out, running through his fingers. The great black eyes with their astonished eyebrows seemed to be staring down at him. Nan walked around the edge of the water, looking into its turquoise depths. The other boat moved off slowly, as if reluctant to end the afternoon. But there was no doubt, it was time.

"You can leave me here," Nan said. "I'd like to live here. At least for a week."

Suddenly Ben let out a yell. "Oh no, it's gone! It's gone. It broke." He held up the empty spool. The orange kite soared above him, free. He put his hands over his face. He thought he was too old to cry.

Everyone stopped moving, except for Brad, whose left hand steadily wound his kite string around the bobbin.

"It's all right," said Brad quickly. "It's not your fault." He studied the reel in his hand. His hands were shaking.

"It was only taped, it wasn't tied," said Marion. "You see? Brad forgot to tie the end." She held up the empty spool to show Ben. "You see. It's not your fault."

"Oh no, oh no, I lost it," cried Ben.

Nicola opened her mouth to say that Ben was bad but she found her mother's hand clamped across her face. Nan watched the kite rise higher and higher. Neither she nor Charles knew what to say. All they could think of was that it was Becky's kite. Sensing tension, Max began to bark.

Marion rescued things. "But look, look at it go," she said. She caught Ben's hand. "Isn't it beautiful?"

There was something glorious about the escaped kite. No one moved. They stood, in a line on the rock, to watch it fly. It went up, twisting with an updraught until you couldn't see its eyes any more, and then steadily, like a bird, sailed before the wind, to the north and east. The box kite brought to earth, Brad finally lifted his eyes to it.

"I can't believe how steadily it's flying on its own," he said, with especial objectivity.

"It's amazing," Charles agreed.

Even the kids were quiet at the sight. Should they cry, or could they laugh? Certainly they felt like laughing, as they stood staring into the air. The wide orange triangle looked more and more alive as it flew away from them. It did not falter, drop or rise, but carried itself straight and true off on a current. It grew smaller and smaller.

"It's a wonderful light-air kite," said Brad carefully. He laughed and patted Ben on the shoulder, a little stiffly. "It's okay, son."

Marion put her hand on Brad's arm. "I

think it's fantastic to see it escape," she said softly. "Don't you?"

Brad didn't answer.

"Did you know Brad nearly didn't bring it," said Marion brightly. Her eyes were wet. "He nearly left it out of the bag."

Ben had gone to his mother, who stood stroking his hair. They were all watching the kite, as if as long as their eyes held it, it was not really gone. Only Brad had turned away.

"Do you think it wanted to get free?" said Ben.

The kite was still visible, but it was so small it was only a speck in the sky. Under it, the boat that had left the next island was getting smaller too. They all stood and continued to watch. Becky's kite, thought Nan, Becky. She'd never met Becky. None of them had.

"We'll wait until we can't see anyone any more," said Ben, cheering up. "Not the kite or the boat."

Brad got busy and brought the other kites in, one by one. The small box, the red and white diamond, and then the third one, the large box. Marion helped, and turned every minute or two to watch the orange kite. It seemed to have been escaping for a very long time. But it did not disappear. Instead, it seemed to rise in the air, to go higher, but no farther away.

"It must have found a current," said Charles.

Nan felt she was standing at a graveside. It had been long enough. "It's gone now. I wonder where it will land?" Someone had already said that.

"Maybe it never will."

"I can't believe how steady it is."

Somebody had already said that, too.

"It's not getting smaller, it's getting bigger," said someone.

"It's changed its mind," said Charles, as a joke, because by now they had given the kite a personality. Not just any personality. It was Becky. The runaway, the one of whom less had been expected, had eclipsed the other tame ones. They were almost proud of the orange kite.

"It's coming back, " said Nicola.

"Hey, it's coming back," Ben yelled down to Brad, who'd left his side now and deliberately, it seemed, had turned his back as the orange spot of Becky's kite narrowed down to invisibility. Brad just laughed and didn't look up. But the others watched. It was not getting smaller. It was getting bigger.

"You know, Nicola's right. The wind must have changed."

"Those other guys in the boat have turned around too," said Ben.

"How can you tell?" Nan narrowed her eyes. True, the small knot of white froth at the end of the boat churned up by the motor was now on the other end. "You're right. They are turning back. They must have forgotten something."

Then she looked up at the kite again. This time, because her eyes had been away from it, she could tell for certain that it was bigger.

"You know, that kite *is* coming back," she said, wonderingly.

They all began to laugh. Nicola was jumping up and down. "It's coming back, it's coming back! We can get it back."

"No, we can't," said Ben. "It won't come back here. It won't come *down*."

"It couldn't possibly," said Marion. "It must have just caught a high current. Sometimes the wind is like that. It's one direction lower down, and another higher up."

They all watched as the kite grew steadily larger in their eyes. Even Brad looked up for a minute.

"It's sure a great flyer," said Brad from his distant position. "I'm really impressed by the way it flies."

They stood. A feeling of wonder spread over the group.

"The boat is bringing it back," said Nicola.

The adults all laughed at that. Brad did not look up.

The orange kite grew larger.

Ben wanted to cry. He felt like it was his fault. He felt sad about Becky, because he knew that Brad was sad. A sadness that never went away was an awesome thing to him. Brad had wrapped up the first box kite now. Ben couldn't tell whether or not Brad was mad at him about the kite. He said he didn't care that it was lost, but maybe he did really. Maybe he was just trying to be nice to Ben. Brad used to be really nice to Ben, and teach him how to play x's and o's. Then he didn't want to see Ben any more. His mother told him it wasn't because Ben did something wrong, but he didn't believe her, especially now. Ben got an ache in his stomach for the thing he had done. He really wished the boat with the boys in it was bringing the kite back. But it was ridiculous. Anything Nicola claimed was bound to be ridiculous.

The boat drew steadily nearer. The kite grew just as steadily larger in the sky. They all stared at it. People started to shift their feet in excitement, and mutter.

"Well it sure *looks* like —"

"What *is* carrying that kite—"

"It's getting bigger."

"It is, it's getting bigger."

Suddenly Ben's desire to cry burst. He began to shriek with joy. "It's coming back! It's coming back!" He jumped and punched his fists into the air. "It is it is it is."

"I said it first!" said Nicola. "It was *me* who said it."

"It *was* you," said Nan, putting her arm around the girl.

They stood like that, Brad and Marion, Nan and Charles, Ben and Nicola, and Max, like a welcoming committee, on the hump of rock as the boat pushed straight through the water, its pointed nose aimed directly at them. More and more majestic, this strange boat appeared. Now it was close enough for the picnickers to make out the man behind the steering wheel, and two boys on the other side, one of them holding the kite string.

"Well I'll be damned," said Brad. "I'll be

damned." He took one look and then went back to packing his other kites in the bag. When the boat got within range, Charles and Ben ran down the sloping rock, calling encouragement. Nan, Marion and Nicola stood at the top, waving steadily as the boat drew up through the little bay, to the edge of the steep rock.

"I'll do the push off," said Ben.

"No, I will." Charles leaned forward and put his hands on the bow to stop the boat from banging its bow. Everyone was laughing and shouting. Only Brad held back.

The moment was formal. The gesture to return the kite had acquired a spiritual significance. The boat driver stood up and said, unnecessarily, "We brought your kite back." They were strangers. The space they each crossed was so huge. It was entirely arbitrary they had met. They were like two trajectories. At this point they intersected.

One of the boys in the boat handed the string to Ben.

"How did you catch it?" said Ben.

"We weren't even trying. There was a big tangle of string floating on the water. All we had to do was reach out our hand."

"It was my fault," Ben confessed, to the other boy. Their eyes met. They could have become friends, if they ever saw each other again.

"It was an old kite," said Brad from where he was.

"But very important," added Marion, so he was not misunderstood.

"Isn't it amazing! Miles and miles of open

water. Who would believe it?"

Nan was talking, but everyone else was talking at the same time. Only Brad was silent. Ben took the kite and walked over to Brad. He put it in his hands. It was another solemn ceremony. The driver put the boat in reverse and began to pull away.

"Are you glad we found it, Ben?" said Charles, his hand on his son's shoulder.

Ben nodded.

"*Not*," said Nicola. She was sulking. She felt Ben had too much attention. "I wanted it to go free."

"Nice people," said Nan.

"Yup, nice," said Brad.

"You've got to be careful with those strings. Make sure it's tied around the spool."

"Not his fault," said Brad.

"The kite ran away, but we got it back," said Ben, jumping around and making it a song. "And it was like a miracle."

"Needle in a haystack, who'd ever believe it," muttered Brad. He took the kite in his hand and started to fold its orange wings. "Good old kite, had it a long time."

Everyone watched his long fingers pleating the cheap plastic around the wooden sticks and sliding it back in the carrying case with the care that is born of great suffering.

The Immaculate Conception Photography Gallery

The Piano Tuner

It was the worst day of the winter. A great wind huffed and sucked along the avenue. Looking out her office window Edith counted herself lucky not to have to go out to work: she had only to climb the stairs to this attic. But the octopus furnace in the basement was unequal to heating the third floor; she'd been shivering over her desk since nine and it was nearly noon. What she wished for, truly longed for, was a hot bubble bath.

It broke all her longstanding rules, to devolve back downstairs into the house in mid-day. When you work at home, as she told her clients, you have to be vigilant. Bathing at noon was one of those indulgences that could become a dangerous habit.

Still. The wind tore plumes of snow from the corners of chimneys, sent sheets of little pellets down from iced branches. Intermittently it hit the window, rattling the pane. Edith scanned the front and back yards. It was an evacuated landscape, sidewalks impassable, cars blanketed and locked in place by ridges of ice. Life was on hold. If she couldn't go down and take a bath today, she would never be able to.

Foam up to her nose, the nape of her neck firmly pressed against the tub, eyes closed, Edith was immersed in the hot water. It was wonderful. Her scalp prickled with sweat and her pores tingled with green pine effervescence. Heaven. Utterly un-Canadian, of course, a flaunting of pioneer ancestors definitely, no doubt regulated against in Methodist churches and perhaps in Ottawa ("Thou shalt not take time off from work for noontime bubblebaths") but worth every feckless moment.

The doorbell rang. She heard it clearly, down the stairs and far away, but clear none the less. The doorbell. Who on earth would venture, she thought. But no matter. She was under no obligation to answer. Normally at this time she was hidden upstairs. Whoever it was did not know her or need her.

Once last month she was caught in the house making coffee by an unemployed tool and die maker selling plastic garbage bags door to door in order to make a little cash: him she had answered to, by sheer fluke. She even bought a hundred plastic garbage bags. But that wouldn't happen again. Today, forget it. Anyway, the bell had ceased.

But now there was knocking.

Edith watched her pink toes rise up out of

the mountain of foam. Her knees had a boiled look. The person at the door was knocking and ringing at once. She did not want to get out of the bath. She did not want to rush down to answer. She especially did not want to appear at the door red-faced and sweating, hair clinging to her scalp, a white terry-towel robe clutched around her midriff.

But people could die out in this weather. What day was it? Friday. She remembered. The piano tuner. Expected at two-thirty. She cursed. Only Mr. Leonides. Only his determined stumbling through the remorseless gale, arriving two hours before he was expected, would force her out of her bath. Sightless, taciturn, once-a-year Mr. Leonides. She had no choice but to let him in, and not to be much longer about it or the man would be frozen.

Edith pressed herself upward by her hands, her elbows bent grasshopper-like behind her back. As she stepped to the mat, the cold air began to jell the soap bubbles on her body. A few swipes with a towel was all she had time for, and the absorbent bathrobe pulled across her back, the belt tied at her waist. The mirror was fogged; for that she was grateful. She made swift wet tracks down the stairs. You can't turn away a blind piano tuner. But oh — the thought stopped her hand on the bannister, her feet in their dextrous descent — at least he couldn't see her.

This mitigating fact in his defence caused her to smile as she opened the door, a smile that would have been lost on him although the forgiveness in her voice must have registered.

"Mr. Leonides! I am amazed you've managed to get here on such a day!" Edith trilled, clutching the two sides of her bathrobe close across her chest against the staggeringly frigid blast that presaged the piano tuner's entrance to her home.

"I was over at Mount Pleasant and Eglinton, and I got a cab," he said, without expression.

He poked his white cane at the doorsill, feeling out its exact height. The tip of the cane entered and slid along the marble floor tiles, its angle growing more acute as he pushed it forward. She wondered what they made those canes of. Was it ivory, like piano keys? Or plastic? Something hard and yellowing, they always looked so old.

Mr. Leonides followed the cane into her house. Behind him she moved to shut the door. Sucked outward to some vacuum created by the exchange of hot and cold air, it slammed. They stood side by side, she steaming, he, bloodless and glazed with snow.

He was a very conventional blind man: although not old, he seemed to have been raised with the humble and rigid expectation of blind people of old, hence his vocation. He wore a tweed cap pulled low over his ears, a nondescript woollen coat threadbare around the buttons and a grey muffler which was crossed neatly over his chest, she now saw, as he undid the coat. He carried a black satchel like a doctor's bag.

She took the coat, which brought her within arms length of him. She was embarrassed. No doubt he could smell the Vitabath, feel her radiating body. The blind were famously sensitive, were they not? The heat fairly blazed from her flesh.

"You'll have to excuse me," she heard herself say, "but I was so cold in my office upstairs that I decided to take a bath."

He merely grunted, following with his face if not his eyes the direction of her arm as she lay the coat on the window bench.

"The piano's just here," Edith said, crossing the living room. "You remember."

Cane out, he approached it. Once the white proboscis met the piano leg he jerked it lightly upward, touching the underbody. Oriented, he laid his cane on the bench. Then, facing the old upright he flattened his hands, and, with his fingers raised like small antennae, began to run them across the top of the piano case.

"People always keep their favourite knick-knacks here," he said.

"Not good for the piano, is it?" she said, knowing. He did not comment. For someone in his profession he was remarkably nonjudgmental. Edith wanted to tell him that: she hated the ones who criticize.

But she was silent, and only watched as his hands fell upon first the old metronome, then a whalebone bird, and then the photograph of her mother, taken before her heart attack. She had been a beautiful woman, and she looked twenty years younger than her age. He picked up the photograph and held it out to her.

"That's precious," he said.

"My mother," said Edith. "It is."

"I wouldn't know," said Mr. Leonides. And because until then he had seemed so free of self pity she did not know what to say. Did he mean he had no mother, or no photographs?

Edith held the photograph in her hands, wondering where to put it. "I had this taken," her mother had said at the time, "because this is how I want you to remember me, *no matter what happens*." As she grew older, preserving the cloud of blonde hair, the dancer's shape, doing the makeup and buying the clothes absorbed more and more of her mother's time until, after the first stroke, she had suddenly ceased to care. She had spent her last few years with matted, dirty hair quite happily slobbering in any old house-dress she could find. It had been a relief to everyone, even to Edith, who had always felt shabby and plain in front of her beautiful mother.

Mr. Leonides made no more personal remarks. Furthermore he had made no response to her confession that she had just got out of the bath. Perhaps this was commonplace. Perhaps all manner of people did this to him, appeared before him déshabillé, taking advantage of his disability. She wondered what tales he could tell.

She was steaming hot, still, although she was drying off now. She put the photograph down on the side table. Having cleared off the case and moved the bench out of range, he had full access to the piano. He stood before its yellowed keys, his fingers splayed wide, testing them for sound. Edith stood behind him. She felt quite comfortable now in her bathrobe, relaxed in fact. She had no thought of testing his blindness: of course he could not see her.

"It's been at least a year since you came," Edith apologized. "And I know the draft from that window is not good for it."

Again he made noncommittal noises. He opened his satchel of tools and kept his attention on the piano, which seemed to settle under his touch.

He had lifted the casing and was absorbed in the workings of the piano. She had never noticed before how intricate, how beautiful the inside of the old instrument was. When she looked down inside the cavity she saw a long, elegant row of tiny hammers. They were wooden, very slim, with curved necks and oval heads. They lay side by side, expressive, submissive, waiting to be struck and to strike in return. Above them the strings shivered.

Mr. Leonides' fingers slid into the cavity; he was gentle; he knew the piano's capacity intimately and he was here to put it in order. He worked deftly amongst the hammers. He opened his black bag and took out tools to tighten strings, glue to shift pads. She hung near him as he worked, hitting a series of keys, and then reaching inside to make adjustments. Edith was conscious of the terry-towel scratching her bare skin. She was aware that her nipples were standing up under the robe.

"Is it very much out of tune?" she said.

"Not too bad," he said in a manner discouraging more chat.

Rebuffed, Edith sat in the wing chair, feet on a hassock, and watched him. Almost by way of rejoinder she allowed her robe to fall open. There lay her forty-five-year-old body. At its very best. Quite pink, from the bath, pubic hair fluffed and curly, ankles crossed. Her legs with their deep side pleat from tennis were good. Her belly was plump but—blessedly—not curdled or dimpled. Her breasts had never been large, which meant that now they could fill out and not collapse altogether. For once, she was pleased with what she saw. Of course, no one looked at this body now, except Edith herself, sideways in the mirror every morning as she dressed. Her husband preferred to make love under the sheets. Her babies were teenagers; years back both she and they had invented rules of privacy designed to end the intensity of their earlier physical connection. And in her consequent invisibility a strange shame, perhaps connected to her mother's extreme fastidiousness, had overtaken Edith.

Still, whether or not one is beautiful, thought Edith, it feels good to be naked with another person. Mr. Leonides, working away on the piano, was company. She considered masturbating but thought he'd hear the noises. She drew the bathrobe off her shoulders and spread it under her—she was still a little damp—as she sat in the chair. She wondered what the piano tuner would say if he knew. Or perhaps he already did know, with his extraordinary senses of touch, of hearing, of smell.

"Would you like a cup of coffee?" she asked.

"Oh yes, that would be very nice," said Mr. Leonides.

While she was up she went to the curtains and closed them: who wanted to look out at all that white and wind? The room was darkened then, so she turned on a little lamp. He would have heard her nearly soundless bare feet on the rug. She passed very close to him. His eyes, partly closed, the iris of one rolled up so that only white showed, the other one glazed over with milky scar tissue, seemed to rest on her.

Edith moved gracefully, consciously, nakedly off to the kitchen to get coffee.

Listening to the percolator, she wondered how one went about seducing a tradesman. According to legend, this sort of thing happened all the time in nearby Forest Hill, if not Rosedale. And a woman she'd heard of in the West End left her husband for the carpenter they'd had in doing renovations. Another story involved a plumber at the cottage and a golf widow. Oh yes, it happened. But how did it begin?

Certainly affairs of this sort put the woman in the driver's seat: it was her house; the man was hired to work for her. If he were to make advances on her it could be taken as a threat, whereas once her interest was made clear his assent could be assumed. Despite Mr. Leonides' awareness of her, Edith did not suspect him of having sexual ideas. It was all up to her. But if she couldn't invite her husband to have sex on top of the blankets, how could she ever make suggestions to Mr. Leonides?

The coffee came down. Time was passing. The telephone rang. It was her friend Sylvia.

"Hi, Sylvia how are you doing?" she said loudly. "Look, I'm going to have to call you back. I just got out of the bath. The piano tuner's here and I've got nothing on."

She assumed her voice would carry down the hall. That ought to take care of it. Without waiting for Sylvia's reply, she went on.

"Piano tuner, yes. He's so sexy. Gotta go." She just caught the beginning of Sylvia's outburst as she put down the receiver.

The sound of keys being struck, sometimes in scales, sometimes singly, met her as she re-entered the living room. Was it her imagination, or was the tuner's voice more commanding now?

"Put the coffee down there; I'll get it in a minute," he said. Mutely Edith snatched the mohair rug off the back of the sofa.

"That draft really gets in under those windows," she murmured. He ran his fingers briskly down the keys.

"Your piano is not in good shape," he said. She stood like a cigar store Indian wrapped in her blanket. "Anybody ever use it?"

"My husband," she said. "But less and less. The children have given it up too."

"What about yourself?" he challenged.

She could swear he could see her breasts as they hung inside the blanket, she could swear he was reading her mind.

"Me?" she said. "I never really enjoyed it."

He put down his cup and returned to work. After watching him for a few seconds Edith tossed the blanket down on the sofa. It was clear that more was needed. She walked behind him, so close as to feel the coarse wool of his trousers against her leg.

"I suppose I should get dressed," she said.

He did not move.

She picked up her robe and headed upstairs. She paused on the landing.

"It's fun to be naked with you," she said. "But don't you think it would be even better if I got dressed up?"

Her negligé drawer held certain flamboyant outfits, bought either by herself in hopeful desire for her husband, or by him, in some similar fantasy while away on a business trip. She chose a crimson satin slip with an ostrich feather boa, powdered and creamed her body first, and brushed her hair, which had dried with a wave in it, and found a pair of fluffy mules for her feet. When she came down again Mr. Leonides had closed the piano case. His satchel was buckled and he was sitting at the keyboard.

"That's done it," he said.

As she stepped up behind him he began to play. He was quite good. Tchaikovsky she thought, it must be: a piece with passion. She was halted by his chords. She listened. He continued past the point of demonstrating that the piano had been fixed. Why did people think the blind had to be tuners? Why not concert pianists? On the strength of this insight she slid onto the piano bench beside him and lay her head on his shoulder.

"How beautifully you play."

He said nothing. But before long he stopped playing and placed one of his hands on her satin thigh. "That's what you went upstairs for," he said. "Tell me about it."

She described the colour (like a humming-bird's throat, she said) and let him run his hands over her breasts, under the thin straps, around her waist.

He was all buttoned up like a mama's boy, his shirt done up to his chin and tucked into his pants, which rode high on his waist. The shirt was flannel, washed to great softness. She climbed onto his lap, facing him, with one thigh on each side of his legs. She arched her back like a cat. Her hips went down on the keys, playing a wide chord. She laughed. He didn't. A blast of cold air hit, giving her goose bumps.

"It's warmer upstairs."

He took his cane in one hand and she took the other. He did not like being led by the hand; he had to know where he was going. She realized that quickly, and stepped behind. "Stairs straight ahead," she said. "Landing coming up in two steps. Turn now." The tip of his cane probed the space ahead of him.

On the second floor he fanned the cane in three directions and chose correctly for the master bedroom. At the foot of the brass bed he stopped, his cane winding appreciably up its posts and over its curlicues.

"I like these," he said, his voice muffled. Edith stood before him. Her lust had been affected by pity. The thought of taking off his clothing, further exposing him to her sight, while he could not see her, was painful but exciting. She began on the top shirt button. But the blind man, showing a certain expertise, quickly spread his suspenders and unzipped his pants, revealing long underwear with a great gaping fly.

"Come here," he said, turning her gently away from him. She sat on his lap on the edge of the bed while he ruched up the edges of her gown and worked himself into her. She felt mildly aroused but more curious than anything: where was the fabled sensuousness of the blind? He no more wanted to touch her than any other man.

Yet now, haltingly, as Edith's gash of red satin wound itself around his greyed white underwear, something did begin to happen. But it was different than what she had imagined, which had run to his hands sliding all over her, memorizing her, sensing her. His need was to be located inside her, to be *there*, with no further logistical challenges.

"I understand," she murmured, consoling him as they made love. Inside her closed eyes she saw the force of the blizzard against the windows, the row of demure, felt-padded piano hammers against the tight strings. She lived again that electrical sensing that began the moment she opened the door with her heat, to his cold.

"Oh Mr. Leonides," said Edith, at one point. He wanted to know how long she had been thinking of this, whether it was every year, or just this year.

"Only today," she said proudly. "Wasn't I clever?"

Afterward, he collected himself admirably until the moment he reached beside the bed and could not find his white cane.

"I've lost my sense of direction," he complained, while she scooted under the bed to pick up the cane: what would her husband think? Going downstairs was more difficult than going up, but once at the door he was eager to be off: he had other calls. She wrote him a cheque for sixty dollars and put her own coat recklessly over the crimson nightgown, donned someone's mukluks, which were stashed in the front closet, and braved the wind to walk him down to the kerb.

"Lovely to see you," she said, "will you be all right like this? Can't I call you a cab?"

"I know where the subway is from here," he said. "Just show me the edge of the sidewalk."

At that point her neighbour appeared with his snow-shovel, and seeing Mr Leonides' white cane shouted that he was getting his car out and could take him to Davisville Station.

"There you go," said Edith fondly. "I'll see you next year then."

"Thank you," said Mr. Leonides.

Only when she went back inside and looked at the newly pitched piano did she miss the photograph of her mother. It was not on the side table where she had put it, not on the carpet, not even inside the piano, where she searched. When the loss came home to her she could not think what to do, whether to fly after him into the gale and demand its return, or to rejoice.

A Travel Writer

At breakfast Angela stared upward.

"Look," she said, "there are helmets in the trees."

She spoke from her table for one. Glazed coconut shells had been wired with light bulbs and hung on the trunks of the palms.

"They do look like helmets," Angela insisted.

The couples and families at the nearby tables smiled uneasily.

Angela was a travel writer. Many mornings when she woke she had to touch the walls to remember where she was. But even that didn't always help. For instance, the white-washed fake adobe her hand met this morning could mean Crete. But it could have meant Santa Fe or Portugal; it could have meant an Andalusian kasbah in North Africa.

But it was Mexico.

Which was of only passing interest. In fact Angela didn't believe in separate places anymore.

She herself did not inhabit geography. She lived on a beam of light, rather like a rainbow but less rosy, an arc, an illumination, an *idea*. She rode her beam from locale to locale, touching down only to see the sights.

On the flight down, as she was riding her beam to Mexico, she had read in *Time* magazine of the death of Gerard Blitz, mastermind of Club Mediterranean. His obituary was sandwiched between that of one of Bette Davis' ex-husbands, and a notice of the forced exile of a ceremonial king of Lesotho. It said that Mr. Blitz got his idea for Club Med while operating temporary rehabilitation facilities for concentration camp survivors after World War Two. This was, in fact, common knowledge, although the literature for this Club Med made no mention of it.

Angela got up to take more cantaloupe and yogurt from the buffet. Waiting in line, she reflected that there *was* something military, something reminiscently fascist about the little square, its loudspeakers, about the way the guests had to line up not just for breakfast but for towels, with I.D. cards around their necks, about the glassily smiling guests who were absolved of all responsibility.

This insight stayed with her as she walked back to the two stifling rooms plus balcony that would be her home this week. Having seen the helmets in the trees, Angela found even *los ballerinos aquaticos* suspect. They rehearsed obsessively in the deep end of the pool, in slick black bathing caps, their nostrils clipped shut, bug-eyed in dark goggles.

They disappeared and then erupted from under the water without notice, saluting. They rolled over like submarines, and their arms and legs flew up as if they'd been shot.

Ten years ago Angela had an affair with a married man. She went on a trip, and he died. Because he was an ordinary man, no Gerard Blitz, she did not read about his death in *Time* while riding her arc of light but in the *Sydney Gleaner* when she came home. Now each time Angela returned from a trip she half expected her lover to have come back to life, to have left a message on her machine saying let's meet on the bike path behind the North Bridge as usual. Usually these fantasies were followed by intense anger.

With Angela in Mexico she carried not only the detritus of her romance but a novel that she had been writing for a dozen years, and to which exotic locales were of utmost importance. In Angela's line of work it was essential to carry something of the kind, if only to provide continuity. This morning she tried to write. It was difficult in the room, which was hot. Even worse at the pool, with the "G.O.'s"—gentle organizers—dedicated to getting you out of your suncot and up playing water volleyball. Angela escaped to the beach, where she mourned behind her sunglasses.

"Angela has been in mourning for ten years," she wrote in the margin of her manuscript, adding an arrow to show where the addition should fit. "David had been about to leave his wife when the head-on collision occurred. Angela was never called to see him, and their secret died at the Emergency Entrance when his heart stopped."

For several years she had tormented herself with the wish that David had been tagged in some way as hers. That, while he lived, she had attached to his ankle, or tattooed in his groin, somewhere his wife would overlook it, a notice that, official identification notwithstanding, he belonged to Angela Waisberg. Then at least she could have rushed to the hospital to see him lying under the sheet that blotted up his dear red blood. She and the wife could have faced off over the corpse.

The beach had flies, and vendors of jewellery pestered her.

After lunch Angela had a siesta in her airless room. At five o'clock she emerged. It was show time. A man called John, from Ottawa, wearing a T-shirt that said "Aging Jock," attempted the hula on the pool-side stage. She lined up with the rest, who tried, with their Sesame Street Spanish, to get the free cold drinks their cards said they were entitled to. But the bar was empty.

Is anyone there? *Abierto?*

Cerrado!

Angela was dining on a terrace looking over a perfect crescent beach, under a matching crescent moon. She had touched the wall that morning and remembered she was on the Great Barrier Reef. With her at dinner were three others—Peter, the resort accountant, Helen, the resort manager, and someone who had come to fix the computerized bar till. Peter told Angela she should look at the white geckoes. Angela thought geckoes were green — they were in Hawaii. It was Peter's little joke: geckoes are chameleons, and they're white because the timber beams they sit on are painted white. Angela remembered live chameleons for sale in little wooden cages in the medina in Marrakech. David, who had been with her (it was the only trip they ever took together), was horrified. He could not tolerate cruelty to animals. The recollection brought tears to Angela's eyes.

Accustomed to the cynicism of travel writers, Helen was touched by Angela's sincerity. They commiserated about white stucco walls. Angela expounded on her theory of the Great International Nowhere: the place that all tourist destinations were being made to resemble, with buffet dinners and paths lit by low discs in the flower beds, and slant roofed "units" for "guests." This place was different, Helen asserted: the National Parks Service was so strict she couldn't plant anything that was not native to Australia. The palms were an issue: they were South African imports. Every now and then the resort was asked to tear them out. But Helen pointed out they were brought to these islands long ago and now seeded themselves. So what is native and what isn't?

"This is the question," said Angela, trying to sound as though her opinion were worth all the free food she'd eaten. She agreed the island was fetching. Helen smiled at the expectation of a favourable write-up, and they got on to other subjects. It turned out she wrote romance fiction as well. She had sent to America for a book on how to. After dinner she read Angela's manuscript. Anxiously, Angela peered over Helen's shoulder.

"Do you think I should take that part out?" she said.

"Yes. It says in the manual that they only like rape when it's by the hero."

Angela could still be shocked.

W aking in the morning with her hand on the wall, Angela realized, for the thousandth time, that David was gone. He was dead for himself and now finally for her. She had long stretches of being dead herself. It was a relief, after the years with David, which she could sum up as involving her being wounded, betrayed and abandoned. She could now only become alive through changes of scene.

After breakfast, a rangy big-chinned fellow was waiting to give her a jeep ride around the island.

"How ya goin', mate?" he said. He wore cut-off overalls and had white hair. His sunglasses flipped up on a hinge. He put his arm over the seat back, nearly touching Angela's bare shoulder, but when she smiled approachably into his face he drew back.

"You might be disappointed," he said.

It was a long, hot drive culminating in drinks at the pool. She told him she was in mourning. "Isn't it interesting," Angela said, "how from obsession one could move into forgetting, maybe even rejecting? By an act of will."

"You got me there, mate," he said.

She *was* forgetting, but it was taking some time. She had a relapse that night. In the restaurant, she spied a tall fellow with acne scars waiting for a table. She rearranged his face, enlarged his chest and then did herself a fast one-minute fantasy that it was David. She even felt her own total bewildered flushing astonishment when he walked over to her, raised his hand to her cheek and said, "Angela, what are you doing here?" She could do that now and then abandon it, like masturbation given up for lack of interest, a decent try but not worth pursuing.

The large and lovely Lisa came by Angela's table as she dined on Maori Wrasse, to inveigle her to sign up for a trip to the outer reef. But Angela had already done the outer reef. It was lovely, but in April the wind blew, the sea was high, and Angela got sick. There was a right time of year to be everywhere and this was not the time of year to be on the outer reef. Instead Angela agreed to take a dinghy to one of the deserted beaches the next day.

The instructions from the redhead at the beach hut were cursory.

"Squeeze the ball, pull out the choke, pull the cord. Wade out chest deep to throw the anchor or you'll beach the boat." He told her to slalom between half a dozen buoys to get out of the bay.

"I hope I can remember all that."

"I hope so too," he said and pushed her off.

Here she was! Driving a boat all by herself in the Coral Sea. With a cooler of lobster and beer! Who needed David? She had a topographical map and instructions to try Turtle Beach, the third one, because no one would be there.

Pristine, deserted, all the brochure words for beaches applied. Angela leapt, rather inelegantly (but who was watching?) over the prow with the anchor and then waded in. She collected the beach umbrella, the lunch cooler, and her snorkelling bag from the dingy and headed for shore. She ensconced herself at the edge of a mangrove cluster, its forked above-ground roots known to harbour crocodiles. The umbrella gave a little trouble, blowing over. Actually it gave her a lot of trouble and she folded it up, counting on her 15 protect sunscreen. They said there was a hole in the ozone layer over Tasmania, which wasn't far away.

She snorkelled over giant clams with big velvety lips, dotted turquoise, purple and gold. They were so erotic, so labile. She ogled the startling royal blue starfish clutched to his bulge of rock like a supernatural hand. She ate the cold lobster, sucked melon, and took notes. How alone she was. How brave. How beautiful the island was. How basic this pleasure was. Well, perhaps a little more complicated than one imagined. She did worry about the anchor, she did run after the rolling, wind-born umbrella, and worry about the boat.

In fact, increasingly throughout this idyll, which was in fact rather short, Angela worried about the boat. Why was it moving in so close to the shore? Was the anchor holding? Would she be able to push it out against the stiff incoming wind and waves, *and* start the motor without flooding it?

Another boat penetrated her beach. She could see from her vantage point two heads, a man's and a woman's. A team of two: one to push the boat out, one to start it. This is what couples were for. And there was no David! Panic set in. Angela decided to leave. She packed up, tried to push the boat out and failed. Well, actually, she didn't try too hard. Because you see *he* was there. A temptation. A man. It was amazing about these temptations. Even on a deserted beach in the South Pacific, off season, when you expected no company save the transparent fish, they arose.

She walked down the beach toward the man. The stretch of sand was longer than it looked, a five-minute walk. She loomed, her intent to invade more and more obvious as they laid their picnic. She felt her figure portentous, one civilization approaching another: Robinson Crusoe meets the cannibals.

"I know why people like us fall in love," she had said to David. "We are both wayfarers and relentless researchers into people. We are *life* cannibals. We eat our own lives." They had barely begun consuming each other, but it was intoxicating. He with his maps of the countries she visited, his tacked-up copies of her itinerary, complete with telephone numbers he never failed to use. She with her spying on his wife, his children, sifting through his wallet when he was out of the room. It was so difficult to give it up that she had continued for some time to drive past the house where his widow lived. In the sense that their affair had been largely about absence, his death had granted her an extra decade to be tucked up in corner couches of expensive hotels devouring memories of him.

When she was within hailing distance the man jumped up and went to fuss with his boat, as if to keep her from approaching the blanket. At least it gave her an opening. And he was a dear, trundled back along the beach with her. He hauled the boat around, telling her the tide was going out, that was the problem. He pushed her off. She started the motor, and Turtle Beach was behind her.

Putt-putting back, she wondered what she would have done if Mr. Helpful had not been there. She would have managed, of course. Perhaps in some desperate way, clinging to the side of the boat, jamming the prop into the sand, screaming in fright, but she would have managed. She felt she had cheated, somehow.

It was a strange atmosphere, on the plane. People were cast about on the rows of seats, the arm rests pulled up, covered with blue fringed blankets so thin they clung like collapsed webs. The passengers' faces were hidden and feet exposed, as if they were corpses dragged in from some battlefield.

Angela had not wanted to go to Japan. She wasn't prepared for this degree of foreignness and as usual it was the wrong time of year. She'd have preferred something easy, the Cabot Trail in Nova Scotia, or a dude ranch outside Calgary. But a travel writer cannot choose her destination. Here she was, on a mostly empty flight to Narita.

The steward had been flying for years. He did the Japan/Hong Kong run and bought stuff for an importing business he ran on the side. Nat said he didn't even bother with Tokyo anymore. He had been flying over Vietnam since the war. He used to look down and see all the smoke and destruction. "Makes you feel funny," he said, "up in the air and out of it all." Now he saw the beaches on the east side and knew this was the tourist mecca of the future.

"As soon as the Americans lift the embargo! It'll be soon. Maybe this year. It's been twenty years now. The beaches are incredible. Perfect for resorts. Defoliated, you see. Nothing there. Agent orange, you know. The jungle's been taken right back."

Angela felt cold. She wrapped herself in the blanket.

"I say you'd have to have it Club Med style, bring everything right in. Because there's no infra-structure there. There's only jungle. Not even any roads any more. You'd have to be totally self-suffi-cient. But that's the place to be," he said. "The Japanese are in there already looking around."

She ended up in his bed in The Winds at Narita. Nat was actually quite a sexy man, which was odd, for a traveller.

"We'll do this just for fun," he said. And it was fun, even if it was a lie. The lie was that you could get to pleasure without going through any-thing more complicated. This was definitely some-thing to add to the manuscript. She lay awake won-dering what the connections were between travel and war, between travel and war and sex.

We came we saw we conquered. Was that correct order? We travel, we fall in love, we declare war? Or is it we fall in love, with an "other," a foreigner, then we make war because they *are* "other"—then, in the detritus of romance, we travel. By conquering, we make homes for ourselves around the world, supine environments ripe for our lavish attentions.

By loving, we instigate wars. By warring, we pave the beaches for travel.

With David she had been the destination, the colony; he the tourist, the imperialist. Of course she told him too much and she gave him too much. Never realizing that it was the unknown in her he valued, she traded her resources far too cheaply, all of Vancouver for a bolt of cloth, a gun. While his words for her were always generous, what did he tell her about himself other than the usual, that his wife was possessive? (I have other colonies.)

She could not believe how surrounded and propped up he was, by people and institutions, how bedecked with reminders of his value his life was. She was the primitive, virgin territory, he the advancing civilization. She had surrendered so easily, weak at the knees at his superior status.

Except. She had held back, though he hadn't known it. Her submission was mostly show. In fact, she never wanted to make a life with him, only to exploit the passion and to be educated, to be discovered. Had he hung around there would have been an independence movement, a revolution. But he died untimely, illusions of conquest intact.

In Tokyo Angela had a friend called Marika. Marika had lived there for twelve years, teaching English. She made a lot of money and lived in a shoebox. Marika took Angela to a bistro in Harijuku. The hostess, Mama-san, thought she was Spanish, had dyed her hair blonde, and when approached, said "si." Greg and Jim joined their table. They'd been in south-east Asia for a decade. They weren't happy with the culture. "The men see women as mere flesh," said Greg, "and the women see men as full wallets."

They walked the narrow jumbled streets of Harijuku with its hostess bars and love hotels vertically stacked, a sight both amazing and depressing. They were both addicted to Asian women. "They know how to make you feel like a man," said Jim. "But you'll never get through to them. You'll never have a real conversation."

"All the men spend their evenings here, they never go home, it's quite accepted. These girls are from poor families..." said Greg, while Jim recited statistics from a *Newsweek* article he had read about AIDS. He had had a shock.

"The Japanese all have condoms," he said. That is what was always said. "There are condoms everywhere. But the article said they don't use them. They don't use them," he kept repeating, as if to himself, frightened.

Hiroshima. The park in front of the Peace Museum was the quietest place in Japan. Schoolchildren in yellow caps were herded in neat lines through the doors. Inside there was a melted bicycle, and a photograph of a person who had been seated on the steps of the bank waiting for it to open; she had been transformed into a cinder shadow. There was a videotape of a man who'd been in school on the day the special bomb went off. The students all lay on the floor and sang their school song as loudly as they could. One by one the voices stopped; his was the last. Why did he sing? he was asked by the unseen interviewer. Because he thought someone would come to help. When no one came to help, for the first time he was really frightened.

Angela had cried before, but not now. She felt peaceful. The statue with arm outstretched said, "It came from the sky." The implication was there was no one to blame. The tour buses were lined up in front.

Aliens

Tuesday after the August long weekend, after their families' invasion and retreat, the women reclaim the cottages. They bury the compost, wash the sheets and hang them on clotheslines between pines, scrape the candle drippings off the porch table, and take the wine bottles to the dump. The men have gone back to the city, to work. By evening, all of Nightingale Bay from Broken Point to Pancake Island is tidy and calm. The women tuck themselves in bed in luxurious solitude in cottages whose lights, seen from the open water of the great lake, look like lost campfires in the wilderness.

By the driftwood lamp on her bedside table, Teresa is reading a novel. She is oblivious to all but the beating of the heroine's heart, when the phone rings. It is her ring, one long and one short. Teresa scoots across the floor, her bare legs cold beneath her nightshirt.

It's Nan, sounding really pumped up.

"What the hell's going on out there?" she shouts. "Have you looked outside?"

Teresa ducks her head so she can see out from under the overhang of the screen porch. The soft corner of the gingerbread trim frames an infinite blue-black sky, as always. Then she sees the gold ball in the distance, high above the next island.

The gold ball is so peculiar that she stands staring, the receiver dangling from her hand. She ignores the diminished chicken squawking that comes from the receiver—Nan going on. The gold ball descends, spreading light; it seems to gather speed. She expects an explosion when it hits the tree-line, but there is none. The light merely glides to extinction. She looks up where it came from. There is another. Another lovely gold ball descending. Then she notices, high overhead, hovering, something black with two blue lights and a red blinker. UFO is what comes to mind.

"It's aliens," she says into the telephone, interrupting Nan's agitated stream.

Teresa is a rationalist, and a Catholic. She would say she doesn't believe in aliens. But they are landing, and they've chosen to do it right here in Nightingale Bay. It is a calm knowledge.

Nan shouts, her voice raucous. "So it's happening up by you, too? There's three of them, no, *more*, here comes another one. What the hell are they?"

The round yellow lights glide downward. Defined by the ruffle of inky trees between water and sky, the bay is overcome by a new light. It is day, in the sky, although night remains in the branches of the trees, around the shore, in the water. It is a sight at once disturbing and beautiful. It reminds Teresa of Magritte's painting "The Empire of Light," where under a bright sky the lamp post is lit and the houses are full of night.

Nan's voice has dropped to a hiss.

"I'm on the floor, can you believe it? I'm praying it doesn't wake up Aunt Beth." Nan's old Aunt Beth was up for a week from her nursing home. She slept a lot and emerged for drinks wearing pantyhose and pearls.

"This is all she needs. They already claim she's lost her marbles. Let her go back there talking about gold balls dropping from the sky and it'll be restraints and Valium forever." Nan giggles. "Wait, I'm getting a cushion."

While Nan settles in to talk, Teresa does wait, one eye on the sky. More balls are coming down.

"Would you believe over on One Tree Mabel's down on her hands and knees on the floor with a flashlight? She's got all the lights out, thinks the Germans are coming to get her. God! What are they doing to us?" Nan's voice pops against the mouthpiece. "I can see about six of them now, these big bloody balls of fire dropping all over, and there's some kind of plane circling—what is it?"

"I told you it's aliens, landing," Teresa says slowly and deliberately. She has not thought to be frightened. This celestial shower is a wonder. Besides, it is fun to be out of bed, talking on the phone, late like this. Normally they all tuck in at sunset midweek. For once in her life, Teresa thinks, she happens to be in the right place at the right time.

Nan keeps going on. She has talked to everyone. "Nobody else thinks it's aliens."

"What does everyone think?" Teresa asks ironically.

"Greta says it's the Americans. They want Canada and they've decided to start with Nightingale Bay."

Teresa hoots. This is the cottage: you take troubles in a spirit of adventure. A broken motorboat or bats in the roof, aliens or a hostile invasion. There isn't a thing you can do about it, so you call the neighbours, sit back and enjoy.

"I told you Mabel's hiding under the bed, she thinks she's back in London during the Blitz."

"And Joy Ann?" says Teresa.

Joy Ann is the other party on Teresa's party line. She is from Kentucky. Everything scares her here: snakes, open water, even wind. When Teresa told her about the carnivorous bladderwort, she even started getting scared of plants.

"Joy Ann said she saw one of them land by her dock—"

"She did?" Joy Ann's dock is visible from Teresa's window.

"But Jim says," continues Nan, "it could be some kind of new insecticide, against the gypsy moths, for instance, that can only be done at night."

"You phoned Jim?" Jim is after all two hundred and fifty kilometres away.

"Of course," says Nan. "Won't you call Fred?"

Teresa doesn't answer. She hopes spray

isn't the answer; it's too banal. She would prefer whatever the frights and inconveniences of Martians or even the military.

"Just listen to that. Can you hear it?"

They hold their breath. There comes a loud cracking sound. A helicopter is directly over Teresa's cottage. She drops into a squat and pulls the inside door shut over the screen. "Jesus!" she gasps. "This isn't funny."

From the floor, she can see through the lower windows out the front. Outside two of the gold balls strike bottom and disappear, while two more appear, high up. She feels awe. What on earth is going on?

"Maybe it's the Iraqis. Hussein strikes back."

"Oh right. Sure."

"Do you think," says Nan, "there's Indian trouble down on the reserve?" It is the summer of Oka. "Maybe the feds are sending in troops."

The click on the line is Joy-Ann picking up. "Sorry," she says. She sounds distressed and distant. "I'm trying to get through to Quinns. Don't be long, OK?"

"Quinns," says Nan dismissively. "They wouldn't tell you if they knew."

The Quinns run the local marina. Right now the cottagers are fighting the Quinns about permission to expand docks. But even at the best of times the marina owners are closed-mouthed with cottagers. They'd chat you up about boat engines or septic tanks, but come anything important they shut down. In crisis all the locals revert to fishermen and trappers, and turn inward to a community, really a tribe that existed before cottagers. In turn the cottagers patronize them.

People like Nan who've been coming here a long time still call Quinn's the Indian marina. Teresa, a relative newcomer, has put the difference this way. Cottagers try to claim the land with a summer's indulgence; they want to be experts; they want to save the Bay from too much boat traffic, from grey water, from overdevelopment, and equally from the local people and their stubborn desire to make a living. Locals just want to live there. If that means bringing in more gas pumps and opening a bar, so be it. They know they can't go backward, so they try to go forward. Their love for the Bay is inarticulate, complex with hatred and fear and fatigue, but determined.

Teresa is interested in locals. The Turgeons and the LaBontes are down at her end of the Bay, which is one reason it is known as the wrong side of the Bay. She called Napoleon LaBonte to come and get rid of the beaver that moved in under their dock, but he told her he couldn't, it was Turgeon's area. "They have territories for trapping," Teresa explained delightedly to Nan.

"Don't romanticize them," Nan said. But Teresa was charmed by the fish fries and the late night fiddling, if not by the giant TV antennas and the crumbling rib cages of old boats.

"Quinns will tell you nothing," repeats Nan.

"I don't care, I'm phoning them," says Joy Ann, and hangs up.

"I guess she needs to phone someone," says Nan.

Joy Ann doesn't have a husband. She was the left half of a divorced couple and she ended up with the cottage.

"Quinn's aren't going to be just sitting there answering the phone," says Teresa after Joy Ann hangs up.

"Probably partying. Pie-eyed," says Nan.

"You sound like Greta."

Sixty years ago Quinn's father kept the first cottagers alive, fixing boats, delivering food, pulling them off rocks in bad weather. He built his house on Pancake Island and brought his family up from Honey Harbour to found the water-borne community in Nightingale Bay. At its peak twenty years ago, it numbered thirty families and had a church and a school on Pancake Island. The hotels and the summer people followed "Snapper" Quinn, by steam boat from the south. He cowed the Pittsburgh steel magnates and Toronto railway barons with his know how, and took their money for small services. Quinn's son drowned at twenty-five but his wife and kids stayed on in the house. Eventually grandson Quinn took over leadership of the little community of year-rounders, reduced by then to the Turgeons, the MacGregors, the LaBontes, the Boutilliers—all originally French-speaking, with Indian blood.

But Quinn Jr., nicknamed "Muddy" after the nondescript and harmless turtle that was related to the brilliantly coloured snapper, delivered no pithy wisdom and no fresh fish. His settlement was modern and unsightly, with dumped motors, and collapsing docks. He had expanded the hamburger service at his shop on Pancake Island, brought over a chip wagon, and offered overnight docking. That led to music on a loudspeaker and drunken boaters going home in the dark, all just across the channel from Mabel and Nan.

Muddy rarely rescued anyone, except the odd picnickers who didn't know how to anchor their boats. Nor did the cottagers think they needed rescue. Second and third generation now, they were brokers and lawyers. They brought politics and city style to the north: instead of fish fries and dances, meetings, circulars, and lobbying were now the glue.

Only an accident, a fire, or a power failure reminded cottagers of their vulnerability. Last summer, a dry year, the three-day-old remains of a campfire sent up a trail of smoke that in minutes became a leaping orange wall. A battalion of locals materialized in the time it took Teresa and Fred to find buckets and get the fishing boat out. She saw them coming, calm in their tin boats, their little barges, their battered power boats. They landed quietly with fire-pumps and buckets and before long a bucket brigade of twenty-five men and women wound over the rock. The cottagers were shaken and humiliated; this display of impersonal caring left them no words. When the fire was out the locals pulled their hats over their pale faces and pushed off in silence. You never saw half of them again.

"I'm phoning Jim back," says Nan. "Phone Fred."
The helicopter's thrashing sounded through the wires.
        "He's having a dinner party," says Theresa.
But she does anyway.

As Teresa stands up to dial, she sees in the southern half of the sky three more fireballs descending
over the lake. Maybe this is a meteor shower? But
then why the planes hovering, and the helicopter?
The helicopter's explosive cracking drowns out the
ring of her telephone at home so that she is surprised when Fred picks it up and says hello.
        "You won't believe what's going on here,"
she starts in, "but these big yellow balls of fire are
coming down from the sky all over the bay and they
keep coming more and more. It's like an invasion of
aliens. What is it?"
        "Teresa?" says Fred. She can hear his
guests chatting and laughing in the background.
"What are you *up* to up there?"
        "They just keep coming and there's some
kind of UFO sending them down and it hovers
right over our island. They're out by Nan's too, and
everybody's hiding under beds, you wouldn't believe it. What do you think it is?"
        "Well," says Fred, and by the tone of his
voice she can tell he's winking over the receiver at
his dinner guests, "let's try to imagine—you've been
through aliens, and American invaders—"
        "Iraqis, Indians, all that—"
        "There's a plane, you say, overhead? Well,

you know, sometimes when parachutists drop they have flares on their feet."

Teresa feels relieved. The puzzle is solved. Of course, that's it. Parachutists coming down with flares on their feet. Good old Fred! The ballooning silk accounted for the lazy gracious fall, the landing for the sudden blackout. It makes perfect sense, except for one thing. Why are all these paratroopers being dropped into Nightingale Bay?

"Military exercise, probably," says Fred. And again Teresa knows he's right. She imagines troops massing along the far shore. Or shores. But the ragged inlets, the dozens of islands in the archipelago aren't made for marching. It seems a strange project, but she supposes you have to get your troops out, exercising, these days.

Teresa thanks Fred, puts down the phone and goes out on the screen porch. The golden balls are still dropping. She's almost used to it now. She would miss them if they stopped. The sky is day-bright. Now she imagines a dark invisible soldier standing above each flare, and above the soldier the parachute, like great extended butterfly wings. She imagines the landing, all the volumes of silk collapsing on the rocks in the dark, the *deepened* dark after the flare goes out. Soldiers putting down here there everywhere. But how are these soldiers ever going to get together, unless they swim? Well, it wasn't easy landing at Dieppe either. Except that here they'll be stuck, each on his private rock. They can't rush forward, attack, or even retreat. How could you ever invade Georgian Bay? For that matter, how could you defend it? That is the whole problem with this country, she thinks.

She wonders about the squatter down behind Loon Island, how he's taking it. He has a temporary dock in the back bay by the nature reserve. He drives around in a canoe with a little motor on it, standing up in the back, dressed in a camouflage suit. Teresa figures he's a Vietnam vet who's run off to this wild lake in Canada and is living out his war fantasies on a daily basis.

She calls Nan back. "Fred said it's paratroopers with flares on their feet," she says.

"I know," says Nan.

Teresa is irritated. She shuts up. You can never tell Nan anything.

Nan is offhand. "I phoned the Quinns and they told me it's flares. It's only an official search and rescue."

"*Oh*," says Teresa. Only a search. And rescue. The night feels too extraordinary for that. At least it must be a very special search! Surely they didn't search this way for just anyone. "Who's lost?" she says. "What manner of person?"

"That's what I said. Quinns wouldn't tell. I figure it must be some bigwig at Bartholomews."

"Maybe there's a maniac or a murderer or something, escaped from Penetang."

They're laughing again. It strikes Teresa how much fun this is. It's hilarious, actually, like an escapade they've all arranged for themselves, an entertainment they've had put on specially. Teresa goes back to bed, because it was warm there, although she knows she won't stay. She puts out her light and hugs her pillow.

It has been a weird summer. At the very first dinner party Greta's husband set a ghoulish tone by asking everyone when they first realized they were mortal. The answers were funny, at first. Jim said he knew because now when he saw a beautiful girl he didn't lust after her; he thought of introducing her to his son. Fred said he'd been going to put the preservative on his new dock when he realized that he'd be dead by the time any damage began to show. So he didn't bother. Nan said she didn't believe she was mortal. Then Mike Klassen, who had cancer, coughed. They'd forgotten him.

Greta drank too much. She started going on about how she heard the Indians were putting up a big hotel complex. "They can build anything they want, you know, they don't have restrictions like we do. People should do something about them. They'll ruin the whole place."

"Why do they have to build on the point? They own all that back land," said someone.

"The same reason you want your cottage close to the water," said Teresa. Greta watched her carefully.

"They don't own any of it, they never paid for it like you and me," said Jim.

Price was a delicate point. There were families who paid a dollar an acre to the Crown in 1910, and others who paid three hundred thousand, five years ago. Most people shut up when you talked price, except for the new couple who told the story of how they'd pried their cottage away from old Mr. Prudhomme. "I don't think he realized what he'd agreed to..." Meanwhile Greta kept on. "The Indians are turning the whole bay front into a slum..."

Teresa was wondering what she was doing with these people. They were city people, big sharks, the kind who used to show up in her town in summer too. Then Jim turned to her and said, "Don't take Greta seriously. It's just talk. I like Indians myself. I used to fly up north every week on the legal circuit..."

Teresa only remembered saying, "You don't buy land with money anyway, you buy it with blood. My grandfather used to say he didn't own the farm, the farm owned him. He'd given the farm the best of his life, he'd be buried there and all his hopes with him."

Yes, it had been a very weird summer, come to think of it. Right after opening up the first weekend, she and Fred had rescued an elderly couple from a drifting boat; the man was wearing a Scottish tam and carrying a bird cage with two budgies in it. Later, on a moonless night, the taxi boat ran into a rock, broke the propeller and had to spend the night drifting. And then when Fred was in the city (he was mostly in the city, that was what she was discovering about the cottage) Teresa's aluminum boat popped two rivets and sank, nearly taking her with it.

All these tales were harrowing, but humorous, in a "what's next" sort of way. They were like little previews of the main event. Near things. Meanwhile, everyone waited for the other shoe to drop. This is the other shoe. Teresa flips her pillow and hugs it again.

The phone rings. Theresa jumps out of bed and runs for it. It is Joy Ann. "It's an official search and rescue," she said. "It's flares and they're lighting up the whole area."

"I know," says Teresa. She begins to let out a long sigh. "Fred told me it was paratroopers," she says plaintively.

"There's no paratroopers. Just flares. The soldiers are all up there in planes looking down."

That is when Theresa has to give up her last fantasy, of soldiers frog-kicking in formation through the black water. And all of a sudden none of it is funny any more.

She sits for a while in the screen porch. The flares are dropping and the helicopters circling because a small boat and an even smaller body are lost in this wilderness of inlets and channels. She imagines the lost person, a speck, perhaps in a frail fishing boat, tossed in the water. Seeing this unfold is like watching *Aïda* in the SkyDome. The vast space, the tiny players, the slow elephants. It was all about scale. What she thought then was, they have to be elephants or you wouldn't know they were there.

On and on the helicopters go, clattering, insistent, omniscient as they rake the air back and forth over this island, the next, over Silver Bay and Deer Island and further out, to Broken Point and One Tree and Pancake where Nan and Greta are, and then moving farther north toward Wild Duck and the South Channel.

Where could the missing person be? Maybe drifted up on some heavily treed island, maybe scratched and bleeding, or with a broken arm unable to move, unable to signal? Or safely tucked on some little island enjoying the aerial opera too? In a daze perhaps, half conscious, thinking as Teresa had thought that it was aliens. Or floating, hanging on to the wreckage, impotently waving from deep water as the flares bloom and die, bloom and die around him?

And *who* could it be? A bigwig? A murderer? A tourist? When people drown around here it is always the locals. Never the cottagers, with their smart-ass kids and too-powerful water-ski boats, their midnight boat races around the outer rocks. But the locals. They are the ones who know the water, they are the ones who have caution bred in. Still there is hardly a local family without its drowning tragedy.

The Bay is savage with locals. Water swallows them. Ice breaks and they fall through with their snowmobiles. The young ones grow up and go to the cities, but the city defeats them and sends them back broken. Then the water gets them. Quinn's community is not shrinking because it's impractical to live on islands; it is shrinking because the water is swallowing people. There are the Boutilliers whose son drowned canoeing, there was the schoolteacher who fell through the ice after his skoot broke down, and the old fisherman Joy Ann bought her cottage from, who died face-down drunk in a puddle on New Year's Day. Is that how they earn ownership? Teresa falls asleep thinking of her grandfather, buried where he'd spent his life's blood, on the farm.

When Teresa wakes at seven, she can still hear the helicopters. The lake is calmer, the wind has dropped. In the light, it has to be easier, she thinks. Maybe the body is still floating. Let them find it soon.

She has a long hot shower. When she comes out, the helicopter noise has stopped. It is a relief and she doesn't let herself think what it means. She goes out and picks mint and makes mint sauce for the lamb she'll serve the girls tonight. Then she walks on the path. She doesn't phone anyone, and no one phones her. The two male hummingbirds are dive-bombing the feeder, chasing each other away. One of them hits the window and falls down, stunned. Teresa picks him up in a strainer, holds him out in the wind, and in a minute he flies off again.

At eleven o'clock she goes to the marina to put gas in the boat. Muddy Quinn's teenage daughter pulls the stiff rubber hose out of the side of the pump.

"I guess they must have found what they were looking for," says Teresa, in a leading way.

"Yeah," says the girl, her face contorted over the gas tank filler hole. "Over by Wild Duck. Guess the motor swung around and got her. She was cut up pretty bad."

It is Nan who supplies the name, Vangie Turgeon. None of them have met her. Vangie was a local but she'd moved away to marry and then come back, alone, at forty. She had been working as a cook at the Inn in the North Channel. Greta said she'd been seen passing the marina at four o'clock yesterday afternoon, going like a bat out of hell in her little fishing boat, pissed off or just plain pissed.

That's ridiculous, someone countered, she doesn't drink as much as you or I.

Well whoever Vangie was, they put on a great show to find her. What a way to go, said someone else.

Teresa begins to think of the search and rescue as a grand finale to the theatre piece that had been Vangie's life. But they had missed the main event; the finale was all they got. Maybe it was all they deserved. Vangie had been invisible, to them. The night of noise and light, of clatter and flash had been a carnival of yet more impersonal caring.

The cottagers heard no news of the funeral: nobody that Teresa knew went. Quinn's teenager never spoke to her again. Even an inarticulate curiosity in Teresa's face made every Quinn look the other way in the marina store.

On the weekend the men came back. Jim said the association ought to do something about what happened. Why didn't they ask us to help? Why hadn't the police given any warning? Old people had been really frightened. There could have been heart attacks even (though Aunt Beth had slept right through). Again, someone said, "Why weren't we asked to help?" It was just the girls here but they could've gone out in their boats.

The English-Speaking Guide

It is Friday afternoon and Elsbeth is taking her mother to tea at the Four Seasons, where she often goes by herself. Her mother has been unhappy; the tea is meant to cheer her up. Elsbeth can always tell when Minna is down, because she gets confused about time. For instance today she thought Elsbeth said three thirty, when she really said two thirty, so that when Elsbeth came to pick her up at the house, leaving work early, which she hated to do, Minna wasn't ready. She still had to change from low-heeled shoes to higher ones, and put on her burgundy felt hat; she got flustered and forgot her lipstick.

Elsbeth snapped, "Come on Mum, I left the car running."

When Minna got into the front seat the fold lines that ran diagonally out from her nostrils down to the delicate jowls spelled disappointment.

Now Minna takes a tight sip from her gold-rimmed china teacup. Her wide-brimmed hat makes her face look too pointed. She looks around the salmon-pink walls, through the cactus plants to the white baby grand in the corner.

"Very nice dear," she says. Her mouth is small, her lips without lipstick the colour of earthworms. They press together, massaging each other, relaying secret messages back and forth.

Elsbeth takes this comment for a complaint. A complaint that Elsbeth may come regularly to such a place while Minna did not. Not when she was a young mother, because they had no money, and not now, because it is a place where women go on their own, and Minna does not go places on her own. She does travel with her husband, however. They have just returned from a trip to India with a group of teachers from Etobicoke, where they live.

"We had tea in Bombay," Minna adds. "In some fabulous palace. We were taken there by the Indians."

"I'd love to go to India," says Elsbeth.

"Oh, it was hot. You have no idea how hot. Even though I wore nothing but those cheesecloth *sacks* you helped me buy, I was drenched." Minna's voice takes on some fibre here, some passion. The corners of her eyes droop and she shakes her head vehemently. Energy comes to her as she recalls her considerable exhaustion. "I could hardly bear to go around looking at things. And of course they want you to."

"The Indians want you to?" Elsbeth asks her mother.

Minna has a piece of scone in her mouth. She chews slowly, deliberately. Elsbeth is forced to watch, waiting for an answer. Eating, her mother's face pulls sideways; she looks a little like a hamster when she eats, furtive about getting what it needs.

"It's not that so much, it's—" Minna looks over her shoulder, about to say something subversive "—well, all of the men just did what they felt like, which was to sit in the hotel lobby and play bridge. We thought—the wives—that we had to show some interest." She raises her eyebrows, and pulls down her cheeks, deepening the diagonal pleats that fascinate Elsbeth.

"Of course," says Elsbeth. It is a dictum of Minna's that men do what they want, making it impossible for women to do what they want. Elsbeth has heard this particular life view since she was very young. She used to think it meant Minna was a feminist. Now she is not so sure. Perhaps her mother is merely a martyr.

"Finally I was about the only one who'd go anywhere. She took me, this girl, this English-speaking guide, to a government emporium. Leather goods and carpets. Stacks and stacks of carpets with the most elaborate designs. Apparently this was not where tourists normally shop; we could buy directly."

"So did you?" says Elsbeth, her desire whetted by the thought of all those lovely carpets.

Minna's face begins to work again. "I just couldn't. I don't know, I'll probably regret it, but—"

"The poor guide," says Elsbeth, inadvertently. She can see it all in front of her.

Minna looks long and hard at her daughter's face. "I think when you go on these junkets the guides have an exaggerated sense of your wealth. We are not rich," she says.

"Well by comparison," says Elsbeth, and falls silent.

Minna bites her lip.

A tall, short-haired woman goes by their table. She is wearing leather boots that come up over her knee, and carries a sack of books. Elsbeth leans out from the tea table and grabs her shirt.

"Becky, have you met my mother?"

Becky stops, turns, fixes on Minna a proper smile.

"Oh, hello, Mrs. Guy. Did you come into the city to visit Elsbeth?"

"Yes," says Minna. Her mouth shrinks. She is shy. Whenever she gets shy she refers to her husband. "My husband and I were in Asia."

Elsbeth speaks up quickly. "How's it going with Rachel?"

"Mac's got her, can you believe it, for the first time in six months. So I'm free for the weekend." Becky, who is big, lifts both fists above her face to cheer. "But I've got a show due next week, so guess what I'm doing?"

"You're crazy." Elsbeth thinks Becky needn't push herself so hard at work for the moment. She has advised her to sit back and let Mac pay the bills for a couple of years: it takes enough energy to be a single mother of a two-year-old. She has said that stretching herself now will only hurt Becky, and Rachel too. But Becky did not heed

Elsbeth's words. Elsbeth doesn't heed them either. Although she is always tired, work is what keeps her going. Becky waves and strides away across the lounge, leather straps slapping the back of her legs.

"What kind of show?" Minna asks Elsbeth, not shy now that Becky is gone. "Everyone you know is making up shows. Reminds me of when you were a little girl. It was the same thing then. Writing plays for your puppet stage. You were always murdering people. Do you still do that, Elsbeth?"

"What? Murder people?"

When Minna asks too many questions at once, Elsbeth answers the wrong one. It is a way of making Minna feel that she is stupid. Instantly she regrets this small cruelty.

"No. She makes radio documentaries. She went to Africa last summer. Rachel had a Zulu nanny."

"Who's Mac?"

"It's complicated," says Elsbeth, filling her mouth with a bit of scone. How can she explain to her mother that Becky lived with Mac for three years, putting up with his various old girlfriends, new girlfriends, boyfriends. Just when she was about to leave him, she got pregnant. She was going to have the child on her own, but Mac decided they should get married. When Rachel was eighteen months, he left.

"Still separated, Mum. Looks like for good."

Minna is not shocked, she can't be. It is going on with the children of all her friends.

"Ought we to regret this development?" she

says, her head wagging. She jests in reference to some implication that she cannot judge, because she is older. But who made this implication? Suddenly Minna looks off.

"As we grow older, the world becomes stranger—"

"—the pattern more complicated," finishes Elsbeth. "T.S. Eliot."

They smile at each other. It is one of Minna's eccentricities to drop quotations. Minna associates. It is how she thinks. You can't say "daffodil" without her saying, "I wandered lonely as a cloud." Elsbeth likes the quotations; by now she has them memorized.

"She probably shouldn't have married him in the first place," says Elsbeth. "There's lots of women having kids on their own now."

"Yes," says Minna. Her lips have stopped working. Her eyes are bright with interest. The tea is doing the trick. Or maybe it's just talking to Elsbeth. Elsbeth knows Minna is hungry for real conversation. Elsbeth would like to give Minna this gift of conversation, but finds it hard. She doesn't know why. "I read something about that. Older women, with careers. They don't even ask. They just get pregnant. Sometimes from a man they meet in a bar. And they don't tell the men. Hit and run. Ships in the night." Minna mulls this over, fascinated and repelled. "What do you think of that?"

"I think it's rather nice," says Elsbeth airily.

Elsbeth was asked this same question only the night before, at a dinner party. Then, she said it was immoral, "the closest thing to rape that can happen to a man," she said. But she's not going to say that today to Minna.

"You see someone like Becky with her kid and you realize that you could manage, if you had to. Mind you, she's just got one. It would be harder with two." Elsbeth has two children.

"Even harder with four," says Minna. Minna had four.

Elsbeth catches her breath. There Minna goes, making excuses for not getting divorced. Let Elsbeth make passing reference to striking out alone, and Minna will do it too. Always competing.

"Those were different times," Elsbeth says.

The waiter comes up with his doily-covered silver plate bearing the bill.

"They put us in the Taj Mahal Hotel," says Minna, getting back to Bombay as they cross the Four Seasons lobby. "It was a lovely hotel. As I was saying, when your Dad went off with the—" her hand goes in circles off to the left of her face "—men, I went all around with this English-speaking guide."

"Did you like her?"

"Yes," says her mother. "She was very sweet but..."

There is a plaintive tone to Minna's voice. This tone and a heavy sigh is as close as Minna has ever come, in Elsbeth's entire memory, to getting angry. Elsbeth sighs too. When she hears her own sighs these days she feels almost nauseous. The sigh is like poison gas escaping. Elsbeth feels that all her mother's pent-up anger has been poured into her, is stored inside her rib cage. Elsbeth's rib cage is very strong, containing it.

"But what..."

They are in the front seat of the car now. Minna suddenly plunges her head forward into her hands. She is absent for a second. Then she lifts her face to stare at the dashboard.

"I was so unhappy. Just so miserable. So. Un. Happy."

Now Elsbeth is on her mother's side, listening, trying to find out what the problem is.

"Unhappy?"

"Those carpets are made by little children. And they all go blind you know, by the time they're twenty. And the guide—her name was Ragnil, or something, she was only a little thing, she made me go out early in the morning and take a ferry across to see the caves of Elephanta. The three faces of Shiva." She shudders. "These pitch black caves. Creation. Preservation. Destruction. With a flashlight." She shudders.

Elsbeth can feel her own shoulders growing tense.

"I just wanted to stay in my hotel room or maybe go and get my hair done. There was a lovely hair salon, right in the hotel. But there she was, this terribly nice girl, waiting. You see I was her job. She had to show me around her city. But I didn't want to see it!"

They are still sitting in the parked car. Minna's lips are open and the inside of her mouth is dark. Elsbeth sees that her mother's mouth is like the cave of Elephanta. The three faces of Shiva.

The three functions of mothers. Creation. Preservation. Destruction. Elsbeth feels frightened, suddenly. Is she hallucinating? Something terrible obviously happened to her mother in Bombay. But she cannot be sympathetic. She finds herself annoyed.

"Why didn't you just tell the guide you didn't need her, and do what you wanted?" It is the old question. Why, mother, didn't you do what you wanted?

Minna presses the button and the car window glides down. Air moves between them, a breeze from outdoors, a reminder they've been lingering. Minna's lips massage each other. She has been challenged. She must defend herself.

"Don't you see?" Minna says, her voice higher and more girl-like. "That would have been ungracious."

Elsbeth's voice is harder this time.

"If you can't even handle the people who you hire to help you, you might as well not go on these trips. You're just going to be miserable," says Elsbeth.

"Oh," Minna cries, "but they were all so kind to me."

"I guess you have to decide what's more important. Being gracious, or getting what you want," says Elsbeth in her tough, lawyer voice, even as she realizes that she has fallen into the trap again. She has given her mother a chance to justify the way she sells herself out.

"And it really was such a lovely hotel," concludes Minna.

Minna wants a good summer walking suit for an upcoming trip to England. She is in the changing room now, behind white shutters trying one on. Elsbeth stands outside, her coat laid on a chair, her hands folded over her purse.

"She really should try the black," the saleslady says. Minna has refused to take the black with her into the changing room.

"I don't think she was fond of the cut."

"You have to see it on. Some of them don't show on the hanger."

Through the slats Elsbeth can see her mother's back, the straps of her brassiere, her wing bones poking between them. The bones are more prominent than they used to be. Her back is curving over the top of the shutters like a question mark. Her head, now disappearing into the blouse, seems larger than it was before, bonier.

"How are you doing, Mum?"

"Oh—" comes the plaintive voice. "I can't get it over my shoulders."

Elsbeth parts the shutters and steps in with her mother. Minna's skin is loose, dropping in folds around her waist, and her stomach has a pouch. Elsbeth remembers how beautiful she always thought her mother was, how vibrant, what a wonderful laugh she had. She adored her mother, still does. But there is something else. It has to do with that body, a childhood feeling of doomed rebellion. She would not be sad, she would not get old, but Minna was always there in front of her, relentless, proof. She pulls the blouse over her mother's shoulders and helps her into the jacket. They step out of the changing room.

"That doesn't do much, does it?" says Minna, her eyes on her image in the mirror.

"It does something. I'm just not sure it's what you want it to do."

"Mmm. And this was how much?"

"This one is really quite reasonable," murmurs the saleswoman, naming the price.

Minna turns her back to the mirror and looks over her shoulder. "See that?" she says, pointing to the hem. "There's something funny about the way it hangs."

Elsbeth looks. There is a wobble in the hemline.

"The fabric. It's very light."

"I think it will crush." Elsbeth knows from the way she says "crush" that this is a final judgement. Minna disappears behind the shutters.

Elsbeth goes to wait by the door. She knows that Minna will buy nothing. It is the usual predicament. The inexpensive is shoddy, the good one too expensive. Minna wants something well made, of quality fabric and design, at a price she considers fair. This desire, not unreasonable on the surface, has led her on increasingly long and fruitless searches. Fabrics and designs and prices are not what they once were. And the salespeople *will* put her off. Making a purchase is a sensitive transaction and not one Minna will enter into with ambivalent feelings.

This search for the perfect suit, in which today's outing is but one foray, has over the years assumed mythic proportions. More curiously the quest has become Elsbeth's. It is up to her, or she feels it is up to her, to secure this ultimate transaction, to *find Minna what she wants*. Why? Perhaps as a compensation for everything that has happened to her mother's life since Elsbeth was born?

But exactly what has happened? Elsbeth often asks herself this question. In 1946, Minna decided against a career as a teacher and married one instead. She had three sons and a daughter, to whom she was a devoted mother, and now she is unhappy. Meanwhile Elsbeth, her solace and her companion, is successful and busy, a mother herself. Minna seems to feel that if Elsbeth, married, a lawyer, a mother, can enjoy her life, she is rejecting Minna. Elsbeth sees this differently. She feels that she is rejected by her mother because she seems to have no problems and to need no help. Elsbeth has everything, after all!

She has a lot, and finds managing it all next to impossible. She needs help or maybe just sympathy, and does not get it. "Elsbeth can cope," is what people say. She has recently become aware of a desire not to cope. Only today she told her friend Phyllis that nobody ever worries about her. Her mother and everybody else have always assumed that Elsbeth can manage. Elsbeth does not think this is fair: she has been living up to this image all her life and has recently become aware that she is a mess.

"So why don't you stage a collapse?" said Phyllis. "Just fall down on your face and scream. *Be* a mess."

Elsbeth considered this for a moment. She

thought about how she would like to fall on her face and refuse to carry on. She laughed a bit and then said, "I couldn't."

"Why not?"

"Oh because they'd— " what would they do? "—they'd pick me up and get all upset and they'd make me go to bed, and Ken would be embarrassed, and Mum would worry and I'd end up having to make them all feel better."

"The trouble with you is you always think of the consequences," said Phyllis. "If you feel like doing it, just do it."

"They had broccoli and meat and some french fries, and banana for dessert," says Nana. She has her Metropass in her hand and is putting on her gloves. The children are sitting on the floor in front of the couch watching *Polka Dot Door*.

"Did they sleep?" says Elsbeth. "How long?"

"Kate one and a half hours, Oliver maybe twenty minutes."

"Good," says Elsbeth. If Oliver sleeps too long, he won't go to bed until nine. Some days she can stand his being up that late, but not today. Not with Minna here too. Minna is just now taking off her coat and holding it out to the side, expecting someone to come along and take it for her. Elsbeth takes it.

"Mummy!" screams Oliver, his consciousness temporarily released from the television by a commercial break. He scrambles across the rug on his hands and feet, stiff-legged, and jumps on her.

"Mummy!" screams Kate, a second later. She takes longer to get to her feet and slips on the rug trying to run. She falls. By this time Oliver has scaled Elsbeth's legs and hangs like a monkey from her shoulders. She is still holding her purse, and Minna's coat.

"Come here, Kate," Elsbeth says. "Give me a hug." Kate makes it to her feet again and lumbers to her mother.

"Mummy, Mummy, can I have a cookie?" says Oliver. He puts his plump hands on her cheeks, and turns her face away from Kate.

"Just a minute," says Elsbeth, craning her neck to see Kate. "How's my little girl today? Did you have a nice time at playschool?"

"Yes she did," says Oliver.

Nana has been standing with her hand on the doorknob. "Are you ready to go?" Elsbeth asks her with a trace of irony.

"Cookie! Cookie!" screams Oliver. Then there is a surge of music from the television and he darts off. With Kate hanging on to the hem of her dress, Elsbeth limps to the coat closet and hangs up her mother's coat. Then she takes off her own. Her purse has dropped on the floor, and Kate has it open and has already found her wallet.

"Kate no, that's Mummy's," says Elsbeth, bending down to retrieve her wallet. Her credit cards and bank cards are spread all over the floor. Kate screams.

"I want it!" Her voice is high and adenoidal. She has had colds all winter.

"I'm putting it away," says Elsbeth.

"I do it!" says Kate. She is about to cry. Kate rarely cries, but when she does, she cries for a long time, unlike Oliver, who breaks into sobs any time he is thwarted and stops in seconds, simply because he has forgotten what it was he wanted.

"There are times when you suddenly decide to sacrifice your wallet," said Elsbeth to Minna.

"Oh no, you mustn't," says Minna, bending down to Kate. At that moment she is her old self, the mother Elsbeth remembers. "Let's put the cards away together, Kate."

"Okay Grandma," says Kate, beaming.

The kitchen is, as always, wiped and clean. The only things on the counter are some finger paintings done by Kate and Oliver that afternoon. Elsbeth turns on the radio, which sits in the breakfast nook. This is how she finds out if Ken will be home for dinner. If a local news story broke late in the day, one that will have good pictures to go with it, he may well be late. If there has been an event on a larger scale anywhere in the western hemisphere, he may have been sent off in a plane. If he's off on a trip he might or might not come home for a suitcase. He keeps one, packed, at the office. Disasters are his specialty. Earthquakes, assassinations, hijackings, the infinite variety of terrible events that befall the globe and its people.

Getting the carrots, potatoes, and salad vegetables from the fridge, Elsbeth listens to the news. There is nothing she judges to be of consequence. A convention of Liberals in Windsor, but they aren't going to send him since they are near the end of their budget. Soon Minna is happily set up at the kitchen table cutting carrots.

"Will Ken be home?" she says.

"Sounds like it," Elsbeth says.

"You're not sure?"

"I can't be," says Elsbeth. "If there is a disaster of consequence while he's on his way to the car, and they call him back, he's gone."

Minna looks sympathetic. This is always dangerous. Elsbeth does not like to be felt sorry for. She does not like Minna to assume that they are on the same footing, prey to the vicissitudes of men. But tonight Elsbeth only thinks how fine it is to have her mother here for company.

"He goes and then what?" says Minna.

"Then I'll only see him on television for the next few days, maybe a week, maybe ten days."

"It must be difficult. When you've worked all day too."

"Oh, well," says Elsbeth, waving her knife. She will make a game of it, an account of it; she will present it to her mother.

"I've got so that I can tell a three-day disaster from a week's worth one. It's all reflected in the newspaper. You know, if the story starts dropping down from the headlines after the first day, Ken will be home soon. If it stays on the front page, in the headlines, for more than three days, then drops to below the fold, he might be gone a week. A ten-day disaster is rare. Even a war isn't worth ten days now. For that you need an earthquake followed by a mudslide followed by cholera and probably civil war."

Her paring knife goes around in circles. She is enjoying herself, instructing her mother in the ways of the world. "You see it has to keep happening: there have to be fresh disasters revealed in the course of the reporting."

Minna nods. "I see." She looks at Elsbeth admiringly. "Keep the ball rolling. The show must go on."

"Something like that," says Elsbeth.

They are silent for a moment. Elsbeth finishes the carrots and comes to join Minna at the table. They open a bag of radishes. Minna picks one up and cuts off the top, then goes around the sides, slicing as if to take the nail off a thumb. Their knives move cleverly, in concert. Minna's face goes into pleats; her lips move.

"What, Mum?"

"Me? Oh I was just wondering if I should have tried on that black suit," she says. "You were so kind to take me to that lovely store."

"I didn't think you liked it much," says Elsbeth.

Minna looks hurt. It happens over and over again. They are close, then at odds. Things are like they used to be, then Elsbeth is no longer her mother's daughter. She is someone ungracious, or selfish, or even just competent, and that means abandoning Minna. Elsbeth used to think, when she became this other person, that she was like her father, the absent, self-pleasing one. But now, Elsbeth thinks with growing hilarity, she is not sure. Perhaps she is another character in the drama. Perhaps she is the English-speaking guide, soldiering on, doing a job, acting on past instructions, despite the fact that no one really wants her to do it at all.

Minna, Elsbeth and Ken are seated around the dining room table. The kids are in bed. It is eight thirty at night. Both women look hungrily at their plates. Minna is very tired, and has been snacking since seven. Elsbeth is completely frazzled and wants only to get all of this over, have a bubble bath and get to bed so she can be half intelligent tomorrow at the office.

Ken arrived home late, bearing roses and a large smile. He was just in time to kiss the children good night, have his scotch, and sit down at the table. Elsbeth has placed the pork roast, rolled and browned, circled with sliced apples, crouching before him. He raises the carving knife and fork.

"Oh Ken, you're marvellous. Elsbeth's really lucky to have such a wonderful husband," says Minna.

Ken puts down the utensils and picks up his wine glass to take a drink. He's not so hungry; he had a big lunch at noon with a government source.

"To Minna," he says. "Elsbeth is really lucky to have such a wonderful mother, too."

And Elsbeth thinks: I am tired of being told I'm lucky. Maybe I am lucky. I don't care. I feel sorry for lucky people. Lucky people can go crazy too and no one even notices. But what she says is, "Can I give you some carrots, Mum? They're very sweet. I got them from that greengrocers you saw out the car window." She is struck while she says this by the guide-like tone of her own voice. She giggles a little. "I bet that's the same place where Ken bought the flowers. They sell fresh herbs, too. I know you're interested in herbs."

Ken finally puts the knife into the meat. "So tell us about Bombay," he says to Minna.

"It was hot."

"Dry hot, or wet hot?"

"Humid. Sunny too."

He still hasn't started to carve. Elsbeth can tell her mother is starving. Ken doesn't realize how hungry her mother is, he never realizes things like that. Normally Elsbeth would now gently steer the activities away from chat about Bombay, which will upset her mother, and toward getting this dinner going, so that Ken and her mother could continue to think they understood each other perfectly. She would say something like, "Ken, please serve the meat. Mum isn't used to eating this late." And she'd say, "Don't mind Ken, Mum, he just likes to interview people." But tonight Elsbeth doesn't feel like performing this social good deed, this translation, one of hundreds of similar translations she provides each day.

She can hear her voice now. With the children: "No Oliver, don't take Kate's stickers. They're *hers*." "Kate, don't hit your brother. Use your words. Tell him to give them back." With her clients: "Mr. Recamier, I'm afraid you're going to have to face financial reality at this point. There's no point getting angry at me. I'm only the messenger." At some point she took on the responsibility of explaining people to each other, as if she, Elsbeth, were the only one who speaks some universal language. It is this enormous task, not her children, her job, her duties as wife and daughter, that makes her so tired.

Well then the solution is easy, says Elsbeth to herself. If Ken wants to talk while her mother waits for her meal, let him. And if her mother doesn't want to tell about Bombay, let her say so herself. Elsbeth will no longer be the English-speaking guide. Elated, she tunes back in to the conversation.

Strangely, Minna is chatting cheerfully about Bombay. "They treated me like royalty. We saw the Prince of Wales Museum, and some hanging gardens, and—"

Elsbeth picks a piece of buttered carrot with parsley on it out of the serving bowl and eats it. Ken and her mother are doing fine on their own. For Ken her mother recalls the facts, not the bad feelings.

"—the caves of Elephanta," Minna is saying. "With this young guide called Ragnil who was just so good at getting rid of the beggars..."

Now Ragnil is to be praised, is she? A glorious feeling of fatigue is settling over Elsbeth. She imagines that she will get up from the table and lie down on the thick beautiful rug made by peasants in Northern China, close her eyes and go to sleep. She begins to smile. She puts her hands on the arm of her chair, and pushes it backward with her feet.

"How did you know I wanted the mustard?" asks Ken. He turns to Minna. "Your daughter's psychic," he says happily.

Elsbeth holds back a split second. Ken and Minna will be shocked, they will fly around in a dither, and put her to bed, and then come downstairs themselves and wonder in hushed voices while she gets some extra sleep. Tomorrow they'll each take her aside and talk it through, they'll both suggest that she take a leave of absence from the firm. But she will never quit her job, not her real job.

She presses down on her hands, raising herself. She takes two steps, to be clear of the sideboard, emits a shriek, and drops gracefully down on her back. Ken and Minna are up from the table now, gasping and grunting, leaning over her, getting water. Elsbeth supposes she should say something, cry or rant, but she really doesn't feel like it. She closes her eyes. She is having a wonderful time.

To The Falls

The boat idles in the middle of a bay. Bob casts. Matthew, his grandson, stands, wobbling a bit due to the instability of the hull, and goes to him.

"Grandpa," he says, "are you going to *play with* the fish?"

In his voice is a slight, barely noticeably pride in knowing this term. This is what men do when fishing. But there is also a hint of dread. It is cruel to play with a fish. He doesn't know if he wants to see this.

René, his mother, wonders who told Matthew about playing a fish. Was it her Dad, in one of his grandparental talks? Her husband Jerome is too gentle to fish. Or has Matthew been reading the books around the cottage?

It is a hot, sunny, summer afternoon, the day the children have been waiting for. The Poitras family, men and women, have at last put aside the tools of their work, carpenter's tools for the former, and cleaning aids for the latter, and are going on a boat trip to the falls. Their plan is to motor down the Niagara River. People say you can get to about half a mile above the falls; you can see the mist. René has packed a very beautiful picnic with pickerel salad and chocolate cake.

Every year the Poitrases rent a different cottage, finding it through ads in the local papers. This one is not as nice as they thought it would be. It is small, and on this part of the river the cottages are crowded up against each other, and a bad odour comes with the west wind, an odour of manure, or sewage, or something else revolting. It is somewhat macabre, besides: the owners left around all sorts of fishing and hunting paraphernalia. There is a book on how to cut up a moose, for instance. There are flies on hooks stuck in the plastic headboard of the double bed.

The idea was to enjoy time together, the grandparents, the children, René and her husband. They've talked about doing this for so long. Now they are all together, and Bob has even brought his boat down from St. Catharines. But the weather has not co-operated, and instead of taking the boat out on the water, they've been working. Jerome has helped his father-in-law scrub the hull, oil the teak, and replace various small screws and nuts. He has done this in his affable, over-eager way, letting Bob boss him around. He didn't learn to be handy from his own father: Bob had no son. René and her mother, meanwhile, have been cleaning and cooking.

Matthew and Ila have been whining and waiting.

But today at last they have decided to go. The weather cannot be faulted; it will be good to be out on the water. Everyone is excited: perhaps that is why there has been this bickering.

"Well I have to hook it first, Matthew," Grandpa says modestly.

"But then will you play with it?" Matthew is anxious.

Apparently Grandpa doesn't like this question, because he does not answer. Perhaps it is a little too close to the point. Before they left home, Grandpa and Grandma had a terrible argument. Grandpa said to his wife, "You're so selfish you won't even let me finish my sentence." Then he said, "You don't know what you're talking about so just keep quiet."

This oafish, rude man is unlike the Grandpa they are all getting used to—the folksy, patient, pedagogical one. René, her husband and children stopped dead in their clattering exit from the porch to hear him. After came the plaintive, uncertain tones Grandma raises in her own defence. Her mother's voice made René's stomach turn, as the black fears of her childhood resurfaced. Wasn't this all over and finished with? Hadn't they stopped by now? They were too old. What could they have left to fight about?

As soon as this argument, which was not intended to be overheard, concluded, Jerome turned on René. It was as if he had been waiting for his cue.

"Where the hell are the lifejackets?" he demanded. His voice had a raw, scraping edge. "And the bathing suits? Let's get this show on the road. What have you been up to all morning?"

"I got the charts," René said, voice quavering despite her determination not to let his anger bother her. She feels that he's not really mad at her, he's mad at Bob, or at himself, for the way he plays the fool. "I borrowed them from Joan next door."

Getting the charts has in fact been a gesture of affection for Jerome. He loves charts, maps of all kinds. René herself is dubious about them. She connects his desire for charts with his aching need for approval. René says such aids only cause you to squint over papers and ensure that you don't pay attention to where you're going. She believes that very few people are able to translate what lies flat on a map into three dimensions, water and land and island in front of their face. Jerome has this knack, but he employs it at a cost: the cost is that he doesn't see where he is. He once drove a boat, not her father's boat thank goodness, but a rental boat, right up onto the shore while trying to read a map. But Jerome has said that it is mad to go through life trying to improvise when others have gone before you and have taken the trouble to lay it out in black and white. In happier moments, they joke about maps, plans and strategies laid out ahead and whether or not one must follow.

Today, however, Jerome does not seem inclined to share a little private joke about maps. He is silent, still scowling. Jerome is a brooder, although you'd never know it at first. "Watch out for those brooders," one of René's friends told her when she was dating Jerome. "You can't read them."

It is Bob who speaks up.

"Why do we need charts? Why don't we just float down the river?"

"We might want to know where to stop," René says, dryly.

The result of all this upset was that they left the cottage in a state, and René forgot—though she hasn't told anyone yet—the picnic that she packed with such care.

Now Jerome is examining the navigational charts while his father-in-law looks on over his shoulder. René slumps in her front seat, looking out the side of the boat, taking no interest in their route. They will go along the river, and the river will wind and it will bulge, and they will get close enough to see the mist. It is magic to the children, and she is sorry that, right now, she can't feel that. She is grateful to hear her mother talking quietly to them: look over there, do you see that cottage with the catamaran in front? Oh, Ila, watch where you stand, I think you should be sitting down in the boat. I don't know how long it will take, but won't it be exciting just looking ahead, not knowing when the falls will appear?

"You see, *Bob*," says Jerome, pointing to where the public access road is shown, "that's where we came down." He says "Bob" self-consciously, still pleased that he can be such pals with René's father. René has the sense that her father has separated her from Jerome, that he has stepped into her space. Bob and Jerome share a light with a slight air of congratulation. Their smoke tails off in the fresh air like exhaust. They have silenced the women with their justified anger. Now they take up the space graciously, as if it has been thrust upon them.

"Well *Jerome*," says Bob, "I'm not so sure."

René listens, swollen with resentment. She detests the way her father says her husband's name. He caresses the name, he makes a fetish of the name. It is downright sickening. Once in a restaurant René heard her father ordering a drink for "my son." He isn't their son; he is *her* husband. Or at least that's the way it started out. But maybe things have changed. Maybe René is not their daughter any more and Jerome is their son. Trades-ies. Good riddance, thinks René. To bad rubbish. She smiles. She laughs.

"You're right. That's where we are. That's where we'll go. I'll leave it to you, *Jerome*," says Bob. He goes back to his fishing line, which he has been preparing. He casts again.

Now sitting motionless in the boat in the middle of the bay, René realizes something. In years gone past she would have been enraged by the way her father spoke to her mother and by the way her mother just took it. She spent all that time coaxing her mother to fight back, insisting that she deserved to be treated better. Her mother agreed; she knew it all. But she was helpless, she insisted: she could not change him, and she could not leave.

Now, for René, the knowledge hits her differently. *That's the way they are*, she thinks. *That's how they behave to each other*. It is a dull, sad knowledge. She doesn't worry about them in the way she had, imagining there was something she could do. Instead she thinks about the bad way she and Jerome fight.

I suppose this is growing up, she says to herself. I fret about my own marriage, not my parents'. Since Jerome is not in the mood to appreciate this joke, she keeps it to herself. She laughs.

They chug on, trolling.

"Mum, when are we going to get there?"

"It's not far. In a boat like this we should make it in under an hour. That's if we're not fishing," she says.

The men do not take the hint.

"There's no more fish in this river anyway," says René. "It's fished out. And if it isn't, it ought to be. I read you can only eat one a year, because of the mercury levels."

They ignore this as a churlish, ill-mannered remark.

Grandma Marie and Ila sit wrapped in each other's arms. Her mother has a red chiffon scarf tied over her head, its long ends lifting off her shoulders in the breeze. Ila gazes up at her, rapt. They are playing finger games. It is a pretty sight. René recognizes the tenderness as the aftermath of one of her father's explosions. This is what her mother did with her, to console them both.

Marie is a touch flamboyant, actressy with

her mouth and the pronunciation of words. You could look at them and think they ought to be in an insane asylum, thinks René. Tinkling away to each other, *because there's no way they can participate*. Maybe that's why people go crazy in the first place. Because they are locked out of the sane world. They have no way in so they stay outside and create a world of games and stories.

René recalls when her mother had a real world. It was made up of the kind of people her father did not like. But they were people her mother cared about, worried about. Even now René still runs into people who say, "your mother's a saint." But when Saint Marie would start to talk about a cousin's sick child or the cleaning lady's marital difficulties, Bob would say, after a few minutes, "All right, that's enough of that." And her mother would be silent.

And René would be silent. Her sisters and her brother would be silent. Why? Why did they let this man dictate what could and could not be said? And what was it about the boy with the club foot or the cleaning lady's life that was particularly problematic for Bob? Just that she had a hard time. She was poor, her people lost their jobs, they drank, they got sick. It was the kind of thing Bob didn't like to hear. He didn't like to know. He pretended, perhaps, that it didn't happen. The world as it unfolded was his. He had taken on ownership. He had taken on the responsibility, so the wrongs were his too. Perhaps he felt he ought to be repairing the twisted feet and the ruined lives of others. If so, he never let on. They only learned that to discuss anyone's bad lot in life was implicitly to criticize Bob.

Her father did not like to be reminded of victims. He liked them; indeed, in many respects, he demanded them. He just did not like mention to be made. Victims were supposed to go along with being victims. To be accomplice-victims. "He hates it when I say ouch," her mother had said, earlier that week, when he jammed a too-heavy log into her arms.

Ouch ouch ouch. But I'm guilty of that too, thought René. I don't like to hear her say ouch either. I feel as if I've been hearing it all my life. She should have said ouch to him, that was it, not to René. Not over and over.

"Why do we have to go so slowly?" René said to Jerome.

"We're trolling," said Jerome, but he wasn't, only Bob was. She could tell by the arch way he said "we" that he was ready to be friends.

"But we aren't catching anything," she said, and he grinned.

René and Jerome. She married him because he didn't have an angry bone in his body, or so it seemed. He also had no interest in defending the way things stood: you could say anything. He didn't defend the world because he hadn't got any unfair benefits. He had worked for everything he had. It wasn't enough, and sometimes he felt she belittled his offerings, what he could provide, compared to Bob. Now when he was angry it was because he felt he didn't get enough *credit* for what he did. And it was only when Bob was around, as if he had to live up to his father-in-law's standards.

"So let's go to the falls!" she says. "We're on holiday!" She turns around to the kids and her mother, suddenly filled with rare energy. "I can't wait to see them."

Jerome puts his hand on the throttle. Bob is silently, slowly, reeling his line in. "Have we got all the lines in?" says Jerome, as if there were a boat-load of fishermen, not just one.

"It's coming," says Bob evenly.

Grandma lets go of Ila and ties her kerchief tighter around her head. Matthew stands up.

"Sit down," says René. She has a feeling what is coming. "We all sit down in a boat."

The line is in. Jerome hits the throttle. The inboard/outboard roars. Everything that isn't bolted down flies back. Grandpa loses his footing and sits heavily in his chair. He laughs. He is surprisingly good-humoured about being bullied, René notices. No doubt her mother should have tried it years ago.

"Told you!" shouts René. The kids and Grandma are holding on for dear life. "You're supposed to sit down in boats!"

Jerome pushes the throttle as far down as it will go. The heavy bow flattens out. They fly down the middle of the widening river. Bob pulls out his flask. Jerome watches, but doesn't take any.

"How far are we from the falls?" calls Ila into the gale.

René points. "A long way!" She throws back her head and lets the wind take her hair.

"I used to worry about how much Dad drinks," René's mother had said to her earlier. "But

I don't any more. There's no point trying to change him. You know, I think he'd be worse without it."

Marie's resignation depresses René. Maybe all older women were resigned. It seemed as if when you got old all the lies you told yourself about your life finally wore through, like old carpet, and there, shining up from the floor, were the ugly truths. No, you did not have a happy marriage. No, you are not glad you stuck it out. No, it's not so wonderful to have the children and the grandchildren around. And you had to add to depression a tedious stream of denying comments.

I will not get that way, René says to herself, feeling the wind. I promise. She looks at Jerome. He drives as though he too were trying to escape something.

The boat flies over the surface of the water. The charts, Joan's charts, lift up and blow into René's lap. They almost fly right out of the boat, but she catches them, one by one. She crouches down behind the windshield and tries to spread them out.

"Jerome, the charts!" she shouts.

"Oh yeah," he says. "Well, while you're at it why don't you find out where we are," he halloos back.

She gapes at him, incredulous. "Are you saying you want me to help navigate?" She is notoriously bad at it. She sometimes forgets whether or not he is her accomplice in this, her friend and ally against all that has gone on in the past. He nods, grinning. Of course he is my friend, she thinks.

"Okay, you asked for it." She stays crouched in the bow. By looking at the landmarks on the river's edge she can just about tell where they are. This looks like the last big bay before the falls. She sits up and peers through the glass.

"Can you see mist?" she shouts to her mother. "Can anyone see mist ahead?"

No one can see mist. The river lies flat and wide before them. There is pleasure in the pounding of the big boat's motor. Its roar precludes answers. Nonetheless, René thinks that soon they'll have to turn around. She watches the shore. Is it her imagination, or are the people in the cottages standing stock still, watching their flight? There were stories. Boats did go over, mostly by accident. Only last week there was a last-minute rescue, some sailors who went too far and were being drawn to the edge. A police boat got them and towed the boat to shore.

"I see the mist," says Ila.

"Is that mist?" Yes it was mist. Mist that had risen so quickly and imperceptibly that it was suddenly all around them. They were in it.

"It's definitely time," says René. She braces her feet against what would be a dashboard in a car.

Jerome does not slow down. He is liking it too much. Everyone is liking it, and they don't listen to René. All of them now, even Ila and Grandma, have their faces to the wind, taking it down their throats. The wind takes the wrinkles off René's parents' faces, and makes their skin look stretched tight, young. They are both handsome, noble people with their eyes on the future. It is how she once saw them. Jerome, too, has the thickness taken out of his countenance. You can see the fire in his eyes. The children have become babies, their faces unboned. The wind narrows Matthew's eyes, and Ila's, bringing tears. René, with her sunglasses, can see how they all change. They cannot see that she too has tears in her eyes.

Jerome keeps the boat flying full out. No one knows what he hears, or sees. "Jerome?" says René again.

When you approach a mountain, it looms above, and you know you're getting closer. When you approach the Grand Canyon, you can't see it at all. If you were the first person to arrive you would never know it lay ahead until you took that the last step up to the edge. Then it opens underneath you. The falls is like that, an inexplicable gap, an unannounced collapse in what's underneath you. But water isn't like earth, it doesn't just go away. It carries itself and whatever is on it over the edge. René puts her head over the side of the boat, into the wind. The water has become knotted and muscular. She looks to the shore. There are no more cottages. But people are running from the road toward the river, waving at them. She watches them with amusement. We're too busy on this boat to wave back.

Only when it must surely be too late does Jerome round the curve, and turn the bow away from the falls. He pulls back the throttle. The bow begins to fall. The ride is over.

"There," he says, gently. "I did that for you."

René knows Jerome can't see her eyes. Her heart is thrashing in her chest. "Hadn't we better speed up a little," she says easily, "to get away?"

Although they have turned their backs on the falls the current is pulling the boat back toward the edge. She looks at the shore and she can see that they are still moving. Twisting her neck she can also see a massive head of mist and water droplets rising ahead of them, from the bottom of the sheer drop.

"My, my, René," says Marie, undoing her scarf. "Wasn't that exciting?" She understands nothing.

Jerome pushes the throttle back down too fast. The engine stalls. In the silence they can hear the immense roar of the falls. Even Bob is sitting alert now, not moving, not wanting to start anything. Jerome gives them all a few seconds. Then he turns the key. The motor catches perfectly, and they start to drive slowly back up the river.

"Now what have you done with that picnic?" he says to René.

The Damaged Heart

Morris was pink, and this was unusual. For the past decade and a half, he had been grey. Grey of complexion, grey of humour, his hair past recall of its former black, his skin grooved and his eyes pouched, as if they had seen too much.

But now he was energetic, there was a lift in his gaze and his rosy lips moved constantly, making words, smiling, tasting. The reason for Morris's (Mo for short, Mao to certain youthful colleagues) improved health was simple. He had a new heart.

By the time the transplant came he had given up, actually. His wife had died. His niece Flo thought he'd been on the list too long; he'd never get one now. Doctors liked to give hearts to people who had years to go. Even if now, at his age, a heart came his way, the operation itself would be a risk.

As nearest relation, Flo had got the call.

"We have a heart," said the careful female voice at the other end of the telephone line. "If he wants it."

"He'll want it."

"Before he says yes, there are some things you should know." Flo listened. What she heard was that this was the heart of a seventeen-year-old girl. Along with three other teenagers she had been killed in a four-car collision at Highways 400 and 88 at three o'clock that morning.

"Oh," said Flo.

"It's not a perfect heart. There's been some—damage."

"Otherwise, why him?" said Flo.

There was a tactful pause. The person in charge of intake hadn't heard that. Then with a note—pride? very faint umbrage?— she said, "Frankly, he's not our first call."

"Meaning?"

"Meaning several people have rejected it already."

"Who?"

"Younger people in need of a heart who can afford to wait."

"Of course."

"The girl had rheumatic fever as a child. And then there was trauma in the accident. She didn't die immediately; her injuries put a strain on the organ," she continued.

All Flo got out of that was the word "organ." It sounded awfully personal: he was her uncle, after all. She continued to listen. The details of the damage were too complex for Flo to digest at that moment, but she understood that with any luck this heart could beat on for a good decade. She stammered her assurances that yes, they should call Morris, and no doubt he would want it.

The phone rang on the morning of a cold, clear November day. Morris put everything on hold and went into the hospital directly. He lay on his back on the rolling bed and looked at the ceiling. As the nurse interrogated him as to his most recent bowel movements and his drinking habits, he mocked her primitive pencil and paper. She ought to have an electronic notebook! Was this a hospital or a museum? Actually what he was thinking was how fond he was of this old town, this old life. Perhaps he would die on the table. When the nurse went away he allowed himself a few nostalgic tears.

Mo, or Mao, was a futurist. He wrote a syndicated newspaper column under the name Dr. Destiny and gave seminars to businessmen on the benefits to be had from the electronic highway, camera telephones and virtual sex. He had started out life as a teacher, had gone through graduate studies in education when that was invented, then sociology when that was invented, and now he just had a habit of sussing out what came next. It was easy to be an expert in the future because most people were so tied up in the past. Not Mao! He embraced the information explosion, audiotext, the interactive television screen as if he had been waiting for them his whole life.

We have to keep company with the new, he was certain of that, and with this certainty he became a leader of those thousands, tens, perhaps hundreds of thousands, who read his columns. He was convinced no one needed technical genius. What people needed to know was how to adapt. For this reason, the column tended toward advice. He got letters: Dear Dr. Destiny, my daughter-in-law wants to communicate with me by e-mail, she says the telephone is an intrusion, what should I do? Dear Dr. Destiny, my dictionary on CD-Rom won't decrunch, what do you recommend? Dear Dr. Destiny, my husband keeps killing women in his Fictional World CD-Rom Adventure Series, should I worry?

He wanted a local anaesthetic so he could watch but they wouldn't go that far. He was saying that he found that archaic and anti-democratic when the anaesthetist came up. He counted up to twelve and was out. But only a few weeks later, he was back in the office, looking so well. Mao, Mao, the well-wishers chimed, pumping his arm, youngsters of thirty-five they were.

Morris himself was stunned. It wasn't just the pinkness of his face, the general good circulation, which made his spine tingle after morning stretches. It wasn't only the spring in his step. He felt younger. He felt yearnings that were so unfamiliar he questioned his doctors about the medication. It was only something to suppress his body's immune system so he wouldn't reject the new heart, he was assured.

The very mention of rejection made him babble. "Oh don't misunderstand me," he said. He certainly wouldn't have rejected the new heart. But there was a process. He had to get used to it, didn't he? That's what Flo said. He had taken to meeting Flo in a cafe for coffee in the mornings before going in to work.

"It *races*," he complained to Flo. She was drinking decaf, but he had found he could go back to a cappuccino, no problem.

"Maybe it's all that caffeine you're taking in," said Flo.

"Not that kind of racing," said Morris. "It's other things set it going." He pressed his lips together somewhat prissily and directed his clear eyes out the window to the street. It was December now but there was no snow. The lamp-posts in this part of town had been festooned with thick ropes of false pine, plastic silver bells and red ribbon. In the pale morning light they looked anaemic.

"Oh do tell," said Flo. She was quick to laugh, quick to cry, a soft-hearted woman and a good manager. She loved her uncle, and she would inherit his company.

"*Dumb* things, like..." twenty-year-old androgynes in jeans with a rip across the thigh, he thought. He couldn't tell her that. "Things I haven't thought about for years," he said. "The full moon last night. Dreadful music by groups with names like Tragically Hip. Sylvester Stallone movies."

"Your heart is young," she grinned.

"Yes," said Mo. "Precisely."

Florence felt briefly jealous. He had

decades on her. She had got used to patronizing him. Now the tables had been turned. Suppose he outlived her?

"My heart is young. That means more than just a fresh muscle," he said. "Have you ever heard of organ memory?"

Florence adopted the sceptical expression that she always wore when Mo dilated on the future. But it was difficult, since she knew that sooner or later people would be taking whatever he said seriously.

"No," said Florence. "Don't tell me."

"Physicians understand that the brain is just one part of the body, one more organ. There's nothing select or exclusive about it. But we assume that only the brain has memories. Wrong!"

He was perched on the edge of his chair wagging his index finger. He was able to bend it at the first knuckle, so that, as he shook it before your eyes, the finger gave the fleeting, bizarre impression of an arrow broken at the tip.

"Your entire body has memories. You know how a dog that has been beaten flinches when you raise your hand? This is not a brain signal, it happens too quickly for that. The poor cur's spine, his ears, his forelegs remember being beaten and that is why, when a hand is raised, he goes into protective position."

"Indeed," said Florence. "Do tell, Dr. Destiny."

"You see, so organs have memories! Kidneys have memories. A liver has a memory. A stomach anticipates a good meal. Genital organs have memories, of course!"

Florence went dead silent.

Mo's lips moved and settled, moved and settled again as he thought.

"They may have memories," remarked Florence at last. "But they have no conscience."

Mo placed his crooked finger on his chin playfully.

"Is that a sexist comment?"

"Why should it be?" said Florence. "I made no distinctions, male or female. In fact, if I were to think about it, I'd say women have less guilt in that regard than men."

"You surprise me, dear," said Mo.

"You used to be old, and now you're young again. You've forgotten about the middle years."

"Anyway, anyway," Mo went on. "It follows of course. What I say now will be of no surprise to you. The heart has its memories."

She nodded. "It has that reputation already."

"*My* heart has its memories. My new heart. The difficulty is, they aren't my memories! My heart, the heart that is beating in me now, has been taken from the body where it lived but it has not left everything behind. In its very beat is the imprimatur of a seventeen-year-old girl."

"And the heart that you had removed? Where are its memories?" said Florence.

"Not altogether lost. I still have my own brain, my own lungs, my own thyroid. But something new has been added. I notice so many changes in myself."

Florence gathered her purse and the check, and stood up to leave. "It's all grist for the mill, isn't it? The body of the future, with its upgraded mechanism. It's wonderful, Mo, that this should happen to you and no one else."

He followed behind, talking doggedly and wagging the confusing fore-digit. "It's a question of what I feel. I feel so strange. It's as if I'm receiving messages in a language I have forgotten."

One of Mo's friends died; he went to the funeral. It was something he did often. This time he enjoyed it a great deal. He enjoyed all the crying, and the fond laughter, couldn't help smiling and giggling as one after another the old folk who were his contemporaries shuffled up to shake hands with the bereaved. Their weighted jowls he found particularly hilarious.

"My, you look well," they said disapprovingly.

Mo had thrown himself into the arms of a man he knew only slightly and liked not a bit and was sobbing on his shoulder.

"I am well," he howled. "I just haven't got control over my emotions."

When he stopped crying he began to giggle. "I'm sorry, I'm so sorry," said Mo. "It just doesn't seem real to me, that George is gone."

They nodded understanding—Mo was not really himself, it was only to be expected, after major surgery too.

Being Jewish, Mo didn't celebrate Christmas. He found it grossly sentimental, and he was frequently churlish in the holiday season. But this year was different. He was touched by the mechanical toys in Eaton's windows; the pealing of church-bells gave him chills; he was shaken to the point of tears when carollers in the shopping mall blocked his exit and sang "Good King Wenceslas" with giant smiles and well-articulated lips. Released, he went away humming. "*Heat* was in the very *sod*, that the saint had printed."

Mo had other new feelings. He wanted to get out, to get away. He took to walking, exploring himself and the city. There was snow, this Christmas. He went into a shoe store on Queen Street and came out wearing Dr. Martens. They were wonderful boots, he discovered; he liked the squeak they made on the dry snow behind him.

His Dr. Martens led him to places he didn't know. The Copa, where the Bare Naked Ladies were playing. He who had never stood in line waited three hours for the doors to open at midnight. With a toque pulled down over his ears and his vigorous circulation he didn't look so very old, he thought. The girls with shaved heads and white falls of straight hair over their raccoon-like eyes looked at him once and looked away. It was not friendly but it was not rejection either, and he was grateful. He took out his electronic notebook and doodled a bit, sent himself some faxes home so there would be something there to greet him. He could call this research. His heart thumped on, happy, and the messages of sadness that he had been receiving, which were too heavy for him to bear, stopped coming.

When he came home the faxes, popping up on his screen after he dialled in, were of no comfort. When he lay down at last to sleep, at three o'clock in the morning, the heart did not want to sleep. It beat on, quickly, urgently.

"Get out of bed! There's no time," said his heart. "The sky is black, shining and clean. At night everything looks brand new."

Though he was tired, he got out of bed and dressed for walking. "You'll be the death of me," he grumbled. "It's not only the ticker you know, it's the back and the legs."

His heart had no mercy. "Outside of Toronto you can see the stars better," it whispered.

And so you could.

He drove to the Kortright Conservation Area. The road was covered with snow. The trees were towering, laden with white, mysteriously creaking under their burden. There was a barrier across the road. Mo parked the car and slid under the bar. His Dr. Martens did their squeaking thing on the dry snow. There was not a mark on it anywhere, only his footsteps.

"*Heat* was in the very *sod*," he sang under his breath. "There's no worry about us getting lost, is there? Police or anybody can just follow my steps."

It had been hard to learn to talk to his heart, it being a girl's and all. He had adopted this fond, indulgent tone.

His heart skipped gaily.

"Don't do that," he complained. "You scare me."

It calmed down. Together they walked down the road.

"My boyfriend used to bring me here in his Dad's pickup," his heart confided. It spoke to him softly, with a lisp, or a flutter, probably something to do with that valve that didn't close too well. He loved the voice of his heart. "There's a place up here where we used to park."

He walked along the curve of the road. He could see tail lights in there. A black Dodge pickup. There was a painful beating in his chest.

"Don't look," he said. "What colour was his truck?"

"Black," she said.

"This one is red."

"I can tell when you lie. You're just trying to protect me," said his heart. He felt a wringing sensation in his chest. "It's him, isn't it? He never loved me!" his heart sobbed.

"There there, there there," he said. "Don't let it get to you," he said. "He's just a kid, you know what I mean? He's gotta live, doesn't he? He's probably crying on someone's shoulder about you. What was his name?"

"Brian," whispered his heart brokenly.

Mao felt a keen intellectual rage at Brian's callousness, sharpened by his heart's soft weeping.

"We've got to work together here," he said. "Listen to me, I am older and smarter."

"That's what you think," it sniffed. "But you'd be nothing without me."

"How right you are!" he laughed. He realized it was not wise to think himself above his heart. He'd been getting away with it all his life. He guessed that the old heart—where was it now?—had more or less given up on him.

They followed their own footsteps slowly back in the snow, Mo and his soft new heart, and drove home. Mo wasn't worried about rejecting his heart any more. He was worried about his heart rejecting him. "You're an old fart, aren't you," he imagined it saying. "I used to drive a newer model."

Mo cried himself to sleep. It was a luxury he'd never before allowed himself. The next morning his eyes were clear and he felt wonderful.

On Christmas Eve Mao went out with some of the young people from his office. They stood in a circle on street corners in Cabbagetown, singing carols. His new favourite was "The Holly and the Ivy."

"Let's do the Holly again," he kept saying, until they all laughed at him. But when everyone kissed goodbye to go home to bed, his heart began to hurt again. "Don't leave me alone," it cried, especially when the young men turned away with their arms around the women.

"You are a sensitive thing aren't you?" he said. The heart didn't answer.

"You wouldn't want me to get in trouble," he scolded. But his heart wasn't speaking to him.

"All right," he said, "all right." He tried the only way he knew to pacify it. He got in his car and drove up to the conservation area.

The pine trees stood heavily in their snow draperies. Again it was a still clear night, perfect for viewing Santa Claus and his reindeer ride across the sky.

"You don't still believe, do you?" he teased his heart. "They didn't give me a four-year-old by mistake?"

He tried to make the turn into the conservation area but the heart started to protest. He eased back onto the highway and kept on going north to Highway 88. "This one?" he said.

His heart was humming now.

It was a century village. The houses were wide solid Victorians made of red Ontario brick. Highway 88 went right through Main Street, past the beer store, the Home Hardware, the antique stores. There was a dark patch, the park, where a shadowy gazebo squatted under bare oaks. The church was stone, with a trio of spires that sailed upwards into the darkness.

"This doesn't look right," said Mao. "You've done something to this town. That's a very old church. Where did it come from?"

"School trip. Northern France," said his heart. "I fell for the gothic arches and the gargoyles."

The cathedral was a great construct, a medieval bishop's wet dream set down there between Lake Huron and Toronto. Mao had never been one for old churches. But that was before. Now, the delicate reaching spires made his heart sing; the heavy cavernous base with its vaulted arches, its open doorway, was like the earth itself. It had belfries and buttresses and pinnacles galore; it was a froth of stone, all glowing gold from a light somewhere. Mo sat at the wheel of his car, contemplating. His heart had stilled. And he was at a loss for a theory.

People might mistake this for a religious moment, he thought. It is not one. It may be spiritual, it may be aesthetic, it may even be hallucinatory. Certainly it is a celebration. This cathedral is a manifestation, a visitation, a virtual something or other...I cannot name it.

Finally, he pulled around to the parking lot behind. There was another car there. He parked and walked into the little field of gravestones.

"I guess we had to do this," said his heart. "Hope you don't mind."

Toward the back there was a cluster of wreaths on the ground. It was the newest set of graves. Of course, he thought, this was the first Christmas without their children for four sets of parents. There was someone sitting on the ground, her back leaning on a stone.

"I can't go closer," Mo said to his heart. "Someone's there."

His heart had begun to bound in a manner that made him fear for its health.

"Please, for me."

"All right, but they're going to wonder who the hell I am."

The woman was middle-aged and wrapped in a ski jacket. She wore a large neck tube pulled up to her chin. She sat quietly on a groundsheet, her head laid back against the stone, nearly asleep. It was as if she'd come for the night. She didn't look at him.

"Is it my mom?" said his heart.

"Short brown hair, glasses?" he said.

"What is the name on the grave?"

He could just make out the fresh carving in the granite.

"Melissa Harper," he said. He was getting a very curious feeling, a sort of clammy chill around the back of his neck. "That's funny, I never said your name before."

But his heart had fallen silent now and gave him no response.

He stood there quietly for a while, before the gravestone. 1977-1993. Such a short life Melissa had. Even her mother could have been his daughter. Underfoot the frosted grass sparkled. When he looked up he saw the stars winking on overhead. Somewhere the old man in his sleigh was riding over the rooftops. An old man who gave things to children. They had it wrong, didn't they? It was children who gave things to old men.

"What are you doing here?" said the brown-haired woman.

Mo's heart skipped, seemed to stop, bled a bit. He did not know what to say. They might have met, that day. It is sometimes done. The families of donors and the recipients keep in touch. Her mother had not wanted to. And there was a time factor, the rush. Mo being uncomfortable. He supposed what it was was that he felt slighted. Perhaps the woman thought an old Jewish man was not a fit receiver of her sweet seventeen-year-old's heart.

"It's not like you have to have me as a son-in-law or anything," he managed.

The woman snorted.

"I suppose if it weren't for me she'd be gone altogether, wouldn't she?" he tried again.

The woman stood up. Her face was gaunt, bleached of emotion, a face that were it not for its strong bones would have been decimated. The face of a survivor.

"I miss her so much," said her mother. "I thought I lost her once before."

"It wasn't fair," Mo agreed. He could not help but feel guilty. He stopped himself from saying that he had nothing to do with the accident.

"I know it's not your fault," said the woman, later, as they walked past the church, which was an ordinary, red-brick church now, United Church, with a lit sign saying Reverend Grindstone officiated. They walked down the snowy street into town. She had cried in his arms, Melissa's mother, there beside the grave.

Once that happened, the rest was automatic. His heart, which had been exerting the strangest magnetic pull, pressed up against the wall of his chest and thanked him. He felt its need. And then it went quiet.

"It's not my fault but I can't help but think you'd rather have someone else," said Mo. "I'm old, I'm bald, I'm paunchy..."

She took his arm. "I know the Chinese Restaurant is open," she said.

The restaurant window was decorated with

gold foil wreaths: Merry hristma was written in a string of letters that hung in a long loop across the bottom. The restaurant was empty. A small Chinese man with spiky hair and an eerie, electric smile popped out from behind a curtain.

"Good evening, Mrs. Harper," he bowed.

"This is my friend Mo. Can we get a couple of beers?"

Mo was revising a theory. It was about *duration*. Organs had memories for a period of time, perhaps; they flashed powerful final signals, and then the chips died.

"You know, Mrs. Harper," he said. She hadn't told him her first name. "How long it lasts is only one aspect of a life," he said. He wagged his forefinger with its one joint bent at her. The waiter stood by. "I'll have chips and gravy, too."

The Immaculate Conception Photography Gallery

The Great White Virus Hunter

The morning Michelangelo was expected to shut down all the computers in the world, Heather sat in the kitchen listening to the radio. She couldn't work; she managed teleconferences for small businesses, her system was vulnerable, and everywhere there were warnings not to turn on. It seemed a bit apocalyptic, but she didn't dare take a chance. There were experts everywhere. Computer viruses, an esoteric subject until two days ago, now dominated airborne chat.

From the long, half-heard radio report, one name detached itself. "Rupert Streath" shot out like a joke, a surprise attack, a roll-up whistle with a feather on the end. Heather sneezed—she had allergies—and her coffee hand froze halfway to her lips.

Then came his voice. Rupert's voice was growly, as if he had something permanently caught halfway down his throat, something he could neither swallow nor spit out. She had not heard his voice in a decade. The sound caught her in the pit of her stomach. Rupert, re-invented in Vancouver as the Great White Virus Hunter. She could see him in his pith helmet. How he must be enjoying this day.

Rupert extrapolated on the dangers of systems contamination. Any user was at risk. The degree of risk depended, he intoned, on the amount of exposure to other systems. Whether you exchanged diskettes; whether you networked with large numbers of users. Oh, viruses were burgeoning—hackers deliberately planted them. It amounted to a technological plague. The costs were going to be enormous, not to mention the security risks, the privacy issues, the disruption of productivity. We were looking at an online millennium.

Rupert was nothing if not a good talker. He discussed the dangers of plugging into unfamiliar networks, and cleaning methods for strange diskettes. If you embarked on computer intercourse, he said you had to use regular hygiene. Now he had the interviewer laughing. He even had Heather laughing by the end of the interview.

Laughing at Rupert Streath, who had disappeared twenty years ago with the kid: she would not have thought it possible. But of course he was still abroad. People like him never really went away. Most of his sort had been reincarnated long ago, members of the Weather Underground becoming stock brokers and primary school teachers. Why not Rupert? When he was in hiding he'd launched that fathers' rights group, putting Heather on his mailing list. But he'd given that up when the custody fight ended. Silence throughout the eighties, and now this. She wouldn't be surprised if he had invented Michelangelo, to give himself something new to fight.

Heather stood arrested at the counter, her coffee cup in the sink, still gaping at the radio. Her impulse was to tell someone. "He's surfaced, I heard him!" But who? She had been reincarnated herself. None of her current friends knew about Rupert. There was poor Marge, red-nosed, stoop-shouldered Marge with her gothic suffering, but Heather was out of touch with Marge too. Marge had found herself a bond trader who retired early to teach skiing in the Beaver Valley. And Cloud, where was she now? Now that her father's fugitive days were over, that Rupert was above ground, now the hunter, not the hunted, where was Cloud? Where were any of them, the children of children of the sixties, with their ludicrous names, like Ché, and Rainbow, and Stormy?

The telephone rang. Heather picked it up.

"Hi!" said a voice. "It's Cloud. Did you just hear my Dad on the radio?"

To love a three-year-old is effortless, and fatal. Effortless because in a child there is no resistance and infinite need; fatal because, for the child at least, absence is death: she will have no memory.

Heather loved Cloud in a way that was total, unguarded and sensual. The love came from constant banal contact, changing diapers, wiping her rubbery cheeks of applesauce, cradling the pudgy silken hand in hers as the toddler jerked along the sidewalk. When Cloud vanished Heather wept. All her attentions— the way she held the squirming body over the bath, the baker's joy of kneading oil into a baby's new skin—would be as nothing. Heather even hoped for this obliteration. Cloud must not suffer; the space Heather filled must be taken up by someone else. Only the presence of love was important.

So Heather had consoled herself, consoled herself and Marge. Marge of course claimed the greater pain; after all, she was the mother. *Mother* became the all-powerful word, once Rupert was gone. Before, he didn't permit Marge to use it. Those were the House Rules.

But that was all Rupert's nonsense, wasn't it? Rupert's line of bull for which both women had fallen, until the trio was exploded and he was gone with the child.

"I did, I heard him."

Heather was laughing, not at the joke of Rupert on the radio, but with joy at hearing Cloud's voice. She didn't ask where she was calling from. There had been years when the phone calls came like this, from telephone booths around the United States. The rule was, if she or Marge ever asked where they were calling from, Rupert would hang up. So you took the miracle voice without question. You were trapped by the spider's silk as it spun out of the telephone, you went still, and hung on, and hoped.

"Did you know he had this business? I couldn't believe it."

"*I* couldn't believe you were still in the house," countered Cloud without answering. So she still didn't answer direct questions. "I looked you up in the book."

"People get to do that if you stay put," said Heather, defensive. She felt as if she had been accused of something—of living in the past, perhaps. This by a child. At first Cloud had been too young to let slip any of the hints they listened for, the names of towns or people, highways or motels. And later she had seemed convinced by Rupert's side of the story, by whatever he'd told her, and was as loath as he to be discovered.

"How old are you now, Cloud?"

"Twenty-three. I've gone back to school. Massage therapy and acupuncture."

"And are you living here now?"

"Why not?" she said.

Heather laughed. "Why don't you come and practise on me?"

The house was not *entirely* the same, Heather said to herself, tidying up the living room in preparation for Cloud's arrival. Well, the same wallpaper of tangled green vines, the same— incredibly, the same— Victorian sofa covered in wine velvet. This room still looked like her grandmother's parlour in Huron County, but that had been part of the fun. But she had stripped the black, gummy stain off the maple trim to show its honey colour and added beige Russian blinds. At least the brooding darkness of the room was gone. She tidied the faded chintz cushions on the window seat, stopping for a minute to look through the leaves to the street.

It was shaded, a dense cover of leaves on the old maple trees overhead. The houses went two by two, respectable, semi-detached Victorians with steep front lawns and rock gardens full of old-fashioned flowers — columbine, portulaca, lobelia. Heather knew the street all too well; she'd grown up there. She had been a high-school student when Rupert and Marge bought the place. She'd walked past on the way from the subway every day after school. She'd seen this dark, bearded man with his orange laced boots painting a sunflower on the stucco next to the front door, and decorating the fire hydrant so that it looked like a mushroom eater out of Carlos Castenada.

Her parents and their friends were scandalized: a *hippie* couple had moved into the neighbourhood. And he was a draft dodger! Where did they get the money to buy the house? What were they up to in there? Soon there were ten or more tenants; no doubt, said Heather's mother, the political convictions of these characters didn't stop them from charging an arm and a leg. Rupert made no friends among his neighbours. Ahead of his time in 1969 he proposed a traffic plan that would have had them all on one-way streets. He came to the ratepayers' meeting to suggest blocking the street to cars; he thought soft drink manufacturers should be forced to take back the containers they sold. The residents resisted but they couldn't deny he had ideas; people still came up to Heather on the street to recall the food co-op and the tin recycling depot.

Heather stopped one day when Rupert was out digging in the front garden.

"What rent do you charge for a room?" she asked boldly. Already she was wearing long gathered skirts made of flowered cotton, a backpack whose straps entangled her long hair, and boots like his. "Is it like they say, an arm, or a leg?"

Rupert had looked up at her kindly from deep socketed eyes; she was stricken. Then, like the cuckoo coming out of the clock, Marge emerged from the front door, babe in arms.

"In your case I'll want it all," he said, before he looked back to his wife. In a remarkably short time Heather had negotiated herself free room and board in exchange for looking after the newborn baby. She went home to tell her parents she was moving out, filled her backpack with jeans and Indian shirts, and walked back down the street to Rupert.

There had been struggles, which she preferred to forget; screaming fights at the gate with Mother, deputations of neighbours, even visits by the police designed to convince Heather to come home. Rupert had been accused of kidnapping, brainwashing, harbouring a fugitive. But in the end she stayed, because she was eighteen and she wanted to stay. Her parents' only comfort had been the fact that at least this man already had a wife.

Heather turned her back on the street, but the room too spoke memories. "I can't believe you still live there," Cloud had said. There were stains along the baseboards still, from where the waterbed stood, here in the front room. Waterbeds did leak. It had been a relief to get rid of it. Pursued by the awakened past, Heather walked into the dining room, where they used to grow marijuana. She'd put in a new floor here; the hardwood was destroyed by the layer of topsoil and humus they'd laid down.

Take the kitchen, which she'd had to redo completely, as it had been Marge's. Clearing out the mudroom where the flattened tin cans had been piled had given her a good-sized pantry, and she stocked it with the tinned tomatoes and rosehip jam she never used. Some of it dated back two decades. The quick tidying tour led her back to the living room, the heart of the house at the time, because that's where the three of them slept.

Supplanting Marge was the last thing on Heather's mind when she moved into the house to take up her babysitting job. Well, almost the last. Any number of freaked-out individuals wafted in and out of the upper floors, part of Rupert and Marge's "family"—the daughter of a couple of motorcycle gang riders who was having a legal name change so she could be called after Halley's comet, some fragile draft dodgers who were apt to cry, a dropped-out architect who planned to build a log cabin in the Selkirks.

But in the family Heather was special. She was younger, she needed Rupert's protection.

Heather had been unconscious of the nature of that protection until he kissed her softly, his big grape lips invitingly obscene inside the nest of beard. He drew her into this same green-papered living room, where Marge was waiting on the queen-size waterbed. After that she'd slept with them every night, in the centre of their love-making. Usually there was one of them on either end of her.

It was a good beginning for a virgin, a full baptism that allowed no holding back. There was only one thing Heather hated. Once she was wakened from sleep by turbulence in the watery mattress; there were Marge and Rupert copulating, hard, banging against each other face to face like there was no tomorrow. It didn't even look like fun. Heather cried until they finally finished. Marge turned her head away and Rupert explained that it was a mechanical thing she'd understand when she got older, that they couldn't really finish up until they did this thing.

And Cloud. What did she remember? Half the time Cloud had been sleeping in the room too, a baby one, two, almost three years old. Cloud was defenceless. But Heather had her weapons. She felt left out of the marriage, she cried to Rupert. And he agreed, if it was going to be three of them, then it had to be fair.

By the way Cloud carried the instruments of her profession Heather was prevented from making cries of delight to see her grown, prevented from kissing her even. She entered in a steam of effectiveness, lugging a folding table with mattress. She filled the centre hall. She was tall without being graceful, even-featured without being beautiful, frizzy-haired, long-necked, just as Marge was.

For a moment she stood very still. Remembering, or not? Her face was made up for concealment, with blue eye-shadow and a slash of red lipstick a camouflage against her real expression. Then she began to move again. They went into the living room.

"Where should I put this?"

"Here."

She went about unfolding the table and set it up, right where the waterbed used to be.

"What were you—ten, maybe, when I saw you last?" said Heather, crowded to the edge of the rug.

"It was when I went back to my mother," said Cloud without looking up.

"Mother" still had shock value for Heather. For years, "wife" and "mother" had been off-limits vocabulary. Though she blamed it on Rupert, it might have been Heather's idea. Or had it been the idea of the decade, to strip Marge of special status, to reduce her to the level of any new woman Rupert chose? It seemed preposterous now, that they had tried to pretend there was no difference between an eighteen-year-old roomer and a legal wife. Even harems have a hierarchy.

In fact, they had all had a hand in dispatching "mother," even Marge. Probably it was a reaction against their own mothers, their fussy, child-like, protected and submissive fifties moms. Or were women only that way in the movies? Could all this have happened because they hated Doris Day?

Once he took up the cause, Rupert made Marge's demotion a moral imperative, of course. There were initiatives and proposals and meetings on the subject of Marge having no special status. (Strange how they never worried about Rupert's special status.) There was to be no sex without all three. No plans made without asking Heather to participate. There were to be no private talks between husband and wife: Heather must be included. Marge was not allowed to hoard the baby at bedtime, bath-time or meals; Cloud belonged to all three.

That part, at least, had been easy. Marge was happy to leave the two children together for most of a day, while she looked after the extended family of sixties lost souls, not to mention the property. Raspberry canes, peonies, snow-shovelling, magnetized her, drew her away from the baby. It was as if Marge's lean limbs and red running nose had to be kept in motion, or the whole contraption they called family would collapse. She would spend hours rigging up a swing from the tree branch, but once Cloud was on the seat Marge would be off to another job. Heather was the one who pushed the ropes forward and back. A year went by, and most of another. One by one the tenants left, renamed or redirected to the Slocan Valley, the Ottawa Valley, to grow strawberries, or plant trees.

When the "family" was gone, Heather thought she would be closer to Rupert, and to Marge, who she loved as much, she thought. But it was then, when they were four, that the house, like an army tank stripped of its disguising branches, emerged as a force. It was Marge and Rupert's house. Heather knew her power by then; she knew she could have whatever she wanted. She'd won already, in bed. Now Rupert entered her first while Marge lay beside, stroking his back. The two women had given up pretending interest in each other; they both tended Rupert.

But sex wasn't enough. Heather brooded over the house: Marge and Rupert had bought it together (with Marge's money). Marge *had* money, you see, from her parents; it was her flaw, it was like original sin: she was born that way and all she could do was strive to better herself for the rest of them. Whereas Marge's money, invested in the Kitchener sewers at three percent (said Rupert) yielded enough for them to live on. It also provided a sword for Rupert to hold over Marge's head—her establishment family.

They had painted and repaired the house, they *dwelt* in it together, with, it seemed to Heather, more comfort, more a sense of rightness, than did she. It was a marriage, that house, it was *the* marriage, it was the secret hiding place of the outlawed marriage. And that was unfair. Because Marge— Heather felt—made use of her ownership. Enthroned at the kitchen table, she planned their meals. She was forever deciding to prune the hawthorn bush, or to repaper the hall. Heather had no attachment to the walls, the rooms, and no right and no money to make decisions. She felt like a visitor there.

A twenty-year-old and a two-year-old playing in the garden. But what a twenty-year-old. Sometimes she sang to the child. "I love you and your mummy doesn't." Heather polished her sense of disadvantage until it shone like a funhouse mirror, stretching and distorting. Heather learned rhetoric from Rupert. She was quicker than Marge, unhampered by the latter's great pain, her lumpen, inarticulate woundedness. Heather had the advantage, fighting to get in, where Marge was only desperately trying to hold ground. By now her fear was so strong it rose like must, like the smell of old dog pee from the carpets, the very walls. Marge was hanging on for dear life, and her only way to manoeuvre was to move even closer to the edge.

When Heather complained about the house, Rupert suggested they go to City Hall and put Heather's name on the title. If they were truly a family, they must all three of them own the house, together: it was only fair. Marge agreed.

But the title change was a turning point. Marge began to fight back. Weakly, pathetically, at first, but cleverly. By then she had realized what she had; she had Cloud. Or, to be more charitable (Heather admonished herself today), the thwarting of Marge's passion for Rupert allowed her, at last, to see her child. Suddenly it was Heather's job to weed the sweet peas while Marge and Cloud went for walks. Heather did the cooking while Marge sat by the highchair crooning to the child. When Rupert was out of earshot, Marge snarled at Heather, "Put my baby down!" Heather began to see that Marge did love her daughter, only a little less stubbornly than she loved Rupert.

Cloud was spreading a white sheet over the thin mattress.

"I'll go out to the kitchen so you can get undressed," she said.

"Do you know where it is?"

Cloud gave her a look. Heather tried another tack.

"Do we have to start this so soon? I thought we'd talk a little first."

"We can have tea after. Are you nervous? Most people are."

"I was just wondering if I should put myself in your hands?" Her voice rose tentatively at the end of her sentence in a way Heather hated, but couldn't control.

"Why ever not," said Cloud flatly and went out into the kitchen. Heather undressed and got under the sheet.

She lay there for awhile. She could hear Cloud in the kitchen, using the phone. "I'm visiting my old babysitter," she said. So that was what Heather was. How simple we like to make our stories. How ordinary we like to make our lives. And Rupert hunted down computer viruses.

Cloud came back into the room. She bent over Heather. Her face was gentle now. The mood had become intimate.

"When did you last see Marge?" said Heather.

"I *see* her." It was mild, factual. "It won't hurt," said Cloud, arranging Heather's limbs under the white sheet to lie flat. "It goes in through the pores and it doesn't even bleed."

"Good," said Heather.

"There's nothing to be afraid of. I use disposable needles too."

"How did you decide to take up this kind of work?" said Heather, attempting to distract herself. The girl was feeling the pulse in her wrists.

Cloud laughed. "It's a long story."

"So's everything. I've got time for it."

"Let's just say that I was a long way from home and I got really sick and someone took me for a treatment, telling me it was going to be a massage, but it was acupuncture, and I was really impressed and so I decided that was what I wanted to study."

Cloud set out little boxes and swabs.

"Where are you going to do it to me?"

"That depends. Where do you have pain?"

Pain was what Marge always claimed. Marge owned pain. When they got to the end, to the terrible screaming fights about Cloud, it was all Marge. "I was the one who gave birth. *I* felt her head breaking through my pelvis. *I* stood the pain."

Heather had been silent. She knew sobbing only turned Rupert off. Rupert was in control, rhetorical, politically justified. He stood in the centre of the room with Heather beside him while Marge threw herself down on the waterbed, sobbing. She rose and fell slightly, with the wave she'd created. Then Rupert told Marge that in order for the threesome to be fair she'd have to agree to divorce him, giving him custody of Cloud.

He loved absurdities and ultimatums. He still kept his tin soldiers. It was predictable with these leftist men, even the ones—especially the ones—who were in flight from the Vietnam war. They all had tin soldiers. Once Heather had come across an essay by George Orwell in which he said that no matter how appealing man tried to make a new world, there would still be tin soldiers. Tin soldiers appealed to some part of man that needed force, and flag waving, and sacrifice. Tin pacifists would not do the trick. Certainly they never had for Rupert. *Catch 22* was his favourite book; he had created one for Marge. If she divorced him, and gave up her rights to the child, he'd stay; if she insisted on staying married, he'd leave her.

"If you don't divorce me, I'll leave you," he said.

Marge wept, and pounded the billowing bed.

The divorce was uncontested, simple. It cost $500, which Marge paid. Rupert insisted on a clause giving him custody of Cloud; this was because, he explained, Marge had been too emotional on the subject. He and Heather couldn't trust her any more. Of course Rupert himself was trustworthy: obviously, he'd never take the child away from her two caretakers.

Heather lay still. It was true, the needles didn't hurt. Not the one in her right wrist, nor the two in her ear lobes. They went in softly at first, by

Cloud's hand, but then she flicked her finger, and something clamped into place.

Heather yelped. "That one hurt." The pin in the back of her right hand sent an electric shock to her collar bone.

"Sorry, I must have hit a nerve." Cloud was kind and rearranged it.

"Agh!" said Heather again. She could have said in her own defence that she'd been young. So young. Younger even than Cloud was today, facing her. She would like to know if Cloud had used that resource of youth to create as much grief as Heather, in her time? Cloud put pins in Heather's earlobes, in her wrists. She asked Heather again where she had pain. Heather wasn't sure. Finally she mentioned the tightness in her lungs, her allergies, her sneezing. Cloud turned her over and pressed on her shoulder blades.

"So you see both your mother and your father," said Heather, gasping on the word father. Heather was pushing the breath out of her lungs. If it weren't for that, she'd have said, "and now you're seeing me." For once Cloud was direct.

"It's not such a big deal you know. All my parents' friends are divorced."

After her victory in bringing on the divorce, Heather was supposed to be happy. Had she been happy? She had been. They let the grass grow tall in the back garden; Heather sat there batting dandelions with Cloud. This was her true youth. She was the child; Rupert and Marge were mother and father, indulgent, sensual. They had even dissolved their union to put her in the centre. She was re-named, like Halley of the comet, reborn. There was no history but this one. There was wet clay earth and Rupert's sweaty smell after digging fence post holes. There was flute music from the verandah at night, beer stew, and flesh tired from work and play. Perhaps happiness was purely physical.

It was Marge who ruined it. How could they laugh when misery stalked by the windows? Heather had to go to Rupert daily with her com-plaints about Marge's behaviour. There were meet-ings; Marge was made to apologize, she was in-structed how to behave, she was reprimanded. She tried to change but she couldn't change the fact that she was desperately sad. In Rupert's war parlance, Marge was the conquered, Rupert the occupier, Heather the collaborator.

But strangely, it was Rupert who broke. Rupert who, finally, had had enough. He was weak-er than the women. Or perhaps he had planned it all. He scooped Cloud, a three-year-old, and ran.

Marge's grief was terrible. She howled, she ran from room to room, her hair stood on end. She got so thin that every time she bent her elbow you expected the skin to tear and a blade to emerge, not a bone. Her nose was perpetually red; she became allergic to all the plants, the fur, the dust of the house. She wrote pathetic poetry about her lost child. She sat in a chair and hugged her knees.

"You don't really own a child," Heather counselled, in the wisdom of the times. "Just be grateful she exists. Think of it as life moving grateful she exists. Think of it as life moving through you. All right, you gave birth. That was your experience. The rest of her life is hers. If she loves you, she'll come back."

Marge rocked on, in physical pain. When she got up finally it was to work on the house. She cleared out the delphiniums and put in roses. She rebuilt the fence. Perhaps she thought that one day Rupert would show up there again, big, black-haired and ferocious as always, with Cloud in his arms. Heather got a job and started night-school in a new field, computer programming.

It was two years before Marge went to court. When the judge heard the story he gave a speech denouncing Rupert. He reversed the custody order, awarding Cloud to Marge in absentia. He ordered Rupert to deliver the child and to appear in court. But as there was no Rupert, and no child, warrants were issued. Just when he became officially a fugitive in his adopted country, amnesty was declared at home. And Rupert skipped across the border a second time.

Marge's private detectives took a long time to track him; in the end the long-distance telephone calls gave him away. He was in North Dakota. Marge and her brother set off, intending to steal Cloud back. But by the time they reached his apartment, Rupert was gone.

It went on and on like that, all of them getting older, until finally the judge gave Marge and Heather the right to sell the house. Rupert being at large, his share was to be held by the court until he showed up with the child.

"Blackmail!" cried Rupert from one of his phone booths. "Feminist conspiracy against men!" "Victory for the monied class!" Heather's father died, and she had money, so she bought the house herself. She saw it as a way of recompensing Marge, although Marge never seemed remotely grateful. Instead she told Heather she was strong enough now to express her hatred. That took roughly an hour, and then she moved out taking her juice machine and her conga drums with her. She believed that the money in the bank, his share of the house, would bring Rupert out of hiding and restore Cloud to her. As it had done.

When Cloud came back in Heather said, "Who were you calling?"

"My boyfriend," she said, adjusting the pin in Heather's ear.

She certainly hadn't come to talk.

"But you're glad to be in touch with your Mum?" Guilt speaking, thought Heather, and winced. But she couldn't help herself.

"She gave me a dog."

"Is her husband nice? I've never met him."

Cloud busied herself with her tray of goodies, and walked the circuit of Heather's table, examining the "points." But Heather couldn't let it go.

"Why did you come?" she said, finally, because she had failed to get Cloud to confide in her.

"Didn't you want to see me?"

"You answer questions with questions."

Heather lay with the pins stuck in her.

"It's the kind of thing women do. We like to tie up the loose ends, don't we?" said Cloud. And then, when Heather didn't answer, she went on. "How did you think Dad sounded on radio?"

"Very convincing. I was impressed."

"Oh he's a genius with computers," said Cloud. "You should see him go in and sweep these viruses out. Amazing."

"I was thinking he'd still like to crash all our systems."

Cloud just laughed.

After the visit, the congestion in Heather's lungs cleared up. She wasn't sure it was the acupuncture. Her allergies were gone. Maybe it had been a computer virus, she joked. She was cured by being away from it one day.

The next day she went up and turned on her system. It was then March 7, 1992. She plugged in her modem and checked her e-mail. One urgent personal note. Seven personal notes. Twelve new discussions in the Webcor conference. She called up the notes, and in the moment before they flashed on the screen she imagined that the urgent one was from Rupert. That he had got into her system, that the whole virus scare had been a way for him to get back to her.

Learning To Swim

At the picnic table on the screen porch six friends are gathered at the end of summer. Their faces are steamed, touched with minute beads of water from the heat, and from the heaping platter of spiced shrimp that has been passed. The sharp essence of pine that lifts the air is momentarily tainted by the odour of someone's steak barbecuing down the beach.

They have all come for dinner and the night at Rayne and Joe's cottage. The Munros have been in France, Max and Ann tried Tuscany this year and Brenda, a music lover, went to the opera festival in Santa Fe. That is where she met Nim. Tonight she is introducing him to her friends. Brenda has been single for fifteen years, raising her son. She sells advertising for magazines. All her friends seem to be blonde. Nim is not blonde. Nim is a black African, educated in England. The sun-bleachedness of the others, their repetitive gold skin and hair is surely an accident, having to do with the time of the year. It has been a marvellous summer, hot and dry. Whether it is greenhouse effect or just good luck no one knows for sure.

"How do you like the heat, Nim?" asks Joe. It is the kind of question his mother asks everyone who does not look as if they came from North Toronto.

Conversation has been jumpy and disconnected. Although a stranger to the rest, Nim with his dignity has been presiding. He brought and prepared the shrimp. He draws the others out, asks what they do and where they come from. He listens carefully, and then deliberately, without seeming to reach, mentions his mother in Africa. How she ran a small shop, how strong she is, at seventy-six. They mention Bruce Cockburn, and he mentions Philemon Zulu, or a writer with a name no one can pronounce. Nim is impressive. He dresses beautifully; he takes business trips all over North America. Nim is adept, accustomed to entering the new element of another culture.

"Oh I find it too hot, too hot for me," says Nim, slowly and politely to Joe. "But we are lucky. The basement is cool. Many nights I must sleep down in the basement. Then it is not so bad."

Nim stands and passes behind Rayne with the painted platter of spicey shrimp. "It is so hot I would jump in the lake, if I knew how to swim."

"You don't know how to swim?"

Brenda breaks in. "He's learning. But he's convinced he's too heavy, that he can't float," says Brenda.

It is like saying he believes in witches. Through the laughter Joe's voice comes, reassuring. As a boy he was terrified of the water too. But he overcame it. Since then he has spent many years in Big Brothers teaching little boys to swim.

"There hasn't been a person born who can't float."

Nim looks sceptical.

"Why didn't you ever learn?"

"I grew up in a small village, only one mile from the sea. But I was never encouraged to go there. My mother said it was dangerous. None of us boys was allowed. Because people who went, maybe they drowned." He reaches for his bottle of beer. "Especially on Tuesdays," he adds as an afterthought.

"Maybe there were sharks."

"More than likely an undertow. And perhaps it came and went with tides. If Tuesday the tide was in the morning, you see there will be a reason to it. There is always a reason for a belief like that," says Rayne. She feels she built up an understanding with Nim while he worked in her kitchen. The others nod.

"It's not too late," says someone.

"I am very heavy in my bones." Nim puts his arm out on the table and puts a thumb and forefinger around his bicep. Everyone looks at his arm, which seems to glow in the lantern light. His muscle is beautiful, like a thick braid. Rayne stirs in her seat; Joe clears his throat uncomfortably.

Nim looks even more serious than usual, in contemplation of his problem. His round cheeks gleam in the candlelight. The pines beyond the screen turn black as the light fails; a breeze is making them bob and whisper.

"You have negative buoyancy!"

"Oh don't tell him that! Don't give him any excuses."

"Do you like the water?"

"I like the bottom. The bottom is my friend," says Nim.

"He loves the bottom," says Brenda. "You should have seen when I met him at the pool in Santa Fe."

"How did you meet him?" says Ann. It is no casual question. They are all curious. How does Brenda do it? How does she contrive to have such unusual experiences?

Brenda grins; she looks like a mischievous twelve year old. "I go on holidays alone, OK? And I love it. I never even notice who else is around. So this time I've been to the opera, right, I've seen the pueblos, it's hot and I'm sitting at the edge of the pool thinking about something profound, my sunscreen, I guess. And I see this man, he comes up beside me and jumps in the deep end. And I'm —" She demonstrates, standing straight by the side of the table, looking down at it. "He doesn't come up. So I'm —" she pushes her neck out and pops her eyes downward at the plate in front of her. "Looking all over the place to see where he is."

She remembers it so clearly: the water is that clear medicinal jelly colour, ten feet deep. The man she will soon know as Nim jumps, a dark jetstream downward among bubbles, he goes down, the bubbles clear. She waits, and there is no man coming up. She looks down and sees him on the bottom, bending over to get on his hands and knees. Then he begins to crawl along the concrete floor of the pool like a baby, this large perfect muscled man.

"She thought I was in trouble," says Nim, smiling at Brenda. Brenda has chin-length straight brown hair and bangs that shake over her emphatic brow. "She was ready to save me but I was not drowning. Then she brought me to Canada and ever since she has been trying to drown me."

People laugh politely. They are not sure exactly what he means.

"I freaked," says Brenda, still telling her story. "I ran around the edge to get to him. By the time I did he'd crawled all the way up the incline to the shallow end. I jumped in and it was only up to my waist; he stood there wiping his eyes. I looked such a fool he had to buy me a drink!"

"I couldn't stay for two seconds down on the bottom," says Rayne abruptly. And although she is meeting Nim's eyes addresses him in the third person. "How does he manage to stay there?"

Momentarily each person at the table tries to work it out. How does he manage to stay on the bottom? By pressing down with his muscles? By concentration, mind over matter? Perhaps he does have heavy bones.

"You must be able to hold your breath a long time."

"Good lungs!" says Joe.

"This is embarassing to me," says Nim courteously.

But it is too fascinating to give up.

"People do have different buoyancies. When I took up scuba diving I was so light I had to wear weights to make me sink. I just kept bobbing up to the surface," says Rayne.

Nim nods. "You see. Some people are light, some are heavy. Easier to be light..."

"Not really. Then you need weights. With weights when you push up off the bottom you don't get all the way to the top. You stop rising, about two feet below the surface. It's an awful feeling."

"I just sink," says Nim. "Can we talk about something else?"

Brenda and Nim put their heads together and laugh, and the others hear her woodpecker rat-tat-tat, and his deeper, restrained roll of mirth. The table separates into two groups as the old friends glimpse a private world, and feel a little jealous.

"So are we doing Scrabble? Bridge?"

"With six?"

"Maybe they don't want to."

They have seen a number of boyfriends come and go. But really they accept Nim. They will invite him, he will be welcome, with her.

"What do you mean trying to drown you? I'm teaching you," Brenda murmurs, her fingers tapping Nim's arm muscle.

They found a place where he could learn, once he came to Toronto. No one asks how it came about that Nim moved to Toronto and into Brenda's house. In fact it was easy and natural. When their time in Santa Fe was up their affair did not feel finished. It seemed there was more to it. He took some time that was owing him and came up. Now he may look for a job.

At Brenda's fitness club there was a training pool, only a foot deep. Nim was very good in there, with all the mothers and kids in diapers. It was only as deep as his knees. He lay on his stomach, put his head up and breathed while his chest was resting on the bottom. Like an alligator, Brenda said. After that he took lessons every morning for a week. He was making progress. But one day he asked the instructor whether, if he found himself in deep water in an emergency, he could manage to save himself. And she said, to be honest, no. He became discouraged. These days he imagines, when he is flying, that the pilot is in trouble and, in case of a crash, is taking the plane over water for a softer landing, to save lives. But this won't help Nim. Nim feels that in this country there is discrimination against people who cannot swim.

Rayne gets up and crosses the verandah the few steps to the kitchen door. Inside is the smell of kitty litter, an overflowing garbage can, a stack of notes left by guests and the kids, borrowing, lending, staying overnight. On the counter is one of Nim's African weavings, a gift he brought, and photographs of Brenda and Nim in New Mexico, at Ontario Place, on the boardwalk at the Beach. She hears the conversation through the open door, while searching for the kettle.

"I think it must be true all Canadians can swim," says Nim. "Because you teach it in schools."

"Can we all, really?"

"*I* never learned in school." That's Joe.

"Lay off, lay off," mutters Rayne under her breath. She calls out loudly. "I thought we were talking about something else." Rayne finds the coffee bean grinder and turns it on. As it gnashes away she finds the kettle. When the water stops rushing, and the grinder is turned off, she hears a commotion on the porch that tells her that her daughter Jo-Lynne and her boyfriend Brian have arrived. There are a lot of hellos and friendly laughs.

"We're talking about how Nim can't swim," says Joe. The kids get right into it.

"Have you tried holding him around the waist in three feet of water, and letting him put his arms and legs out?"

Rayne comes out of the kitchen. Brian is standing beside the table, demonstrating the hold.

"Oh I hated that!" cries Jo-Lynne. "Oh don't you remember how when I was a kid? And Mum always said lie back in my arms, trust me, lie back and relax, sleep. Honest, I won't let you go! And then she let me go."

"—and you get water up your nose—" Brian says.

"—and go under and then she lifts you up and says—"

"—good girl!"

"It happened to you too?"

"Everyone!"

"Is it any wonder we don't trust people?" says Ann, slowly. As she hardly ever says anything in a group the remark settles slowly on them all.

Behind Rayne the coffee is slowly dripping through the filter into the glass pot.

After coffee people sprawl back in wicker chairs; the sunset is imminent but the air still hot. "We could go down to the dock for a swim," says someone.

"Let's," says Brenda.

"We don't jump off that dock at night," says Joe. "Not since the guy next door did and landed on an otter. Boy, did he get bit." He is a little proud of introducing this note of danger associated with his summer cottage.

"Go round to the little beach at the inlet," says Rayne. "It's sandy there, and safe."

Nim gets his suit and towel; Brenda will go skinny. The others stay on the porch talking. Patient, gentle Nim is a little quiet now, perhaps he has been offended in some way. Brenda also says nothing.

When they get to the beach she drops her towel, walks straight ahead and dives in, telling Nim that it is shallow a long way out. He sees her little round head going away. He wants to wade in but thinks he might just as well wait until she is back within range. As she's coming back he steps into the water. He takes a few steps. It is suddenly deep.

Brenda sees him go down. And this time she knows he's in trouble. Without a sound. That's how drowning people do it, they don't make a sound. He simply drops, like a parachutist, his hands over his head. She throws her arms straight up and thrusts herself down, then forward, underwater.

"Why did they lie?" shrieks something in Nim's head. It's too deep for him here. He heads for his trusty friend, the bottom. His feet touch it. He can crawl back to shore. But his friend betrays him this time. The bottom is very soft. As his feet step on it, it just goes away, it floats up around his ankles. He begins to thrash his arms and manages to get to the surface. But he doesn't get a proper breath before he begins to go down again.

Brenda meets him, under the surface, sinking. She puts her hands under his feet and pushes him up. He bursts through the surface and gets one good breath. Then he goes down again. She's still down there, trying to get up, desperate for a breath now. He tries to grab her neck. He has panicked. He's dangerous.

Is it any wonder we don't trust people? Brenda sees Nim thrashing. His eyes are huge, his fingers like claws. She realizes she has to get away from him.

She escapes his grasp, breaks through the surface, catches a breath and frog-kicks herself a metre distant. Then she dives to look. He has sunk farther this time and his legs are bent and tangled on the dark bottom. For one moment she thinks, he is too heavy, I can't do this, I'd better go back and get the others. But he sees her, she knows he sees her. I am afraid, this is total fear, I can't get him, but I must get him.

Somehow Brenda shoots toward him along the bottom and puts her arms around his calves. His arms are going like mad, trying to get hold of anything and take it down with him, even if it is Brenda. She has the strange feeling that he blames her, he is angry at her.

She stays low, squeezes his calves, braces her feet in the squishy bottom and boosts him up and toward the shore. Her lungs are about to crack. But that push gets him to the top again, long enough to catch a breath. She can't believe how heavy he is. He sinks again, and if a stone could flail that would be him. As he is going down she is trying to go up, and she is certain he wants to drown her. She evades him and bursts through the glass surface again, gets a breath in the black air, from which all light has now departed, and dives again.

The water holds the last beams of light. She can see his face down there, grey, looking up at her. He seems to be blurring, as if he were already dead, as if she has already let go of him for good. He is a man she loves, or he was a man she loved. Some tense has been crossed, they are one remove of time from what they were. Their eyes meet, make a line between them. And something changes. Nim still flails, but he does not reach. She knows now he will not interfere with her. She shoots down under him again.

They get a rhythm going. Brenda gets beneath him, pushing him up and then shooting out of his reach, because even now that they both understand what is needed, he could pull her down. She takes a breath, he takes a breath, and they go down together. They just keep doing that, as if they are bouncing on a huge soft trampoline. After four bounces they are back on a firm bottom. They stagger to shore.

Nim coughs. Bends over his bare wet legs and hacks, spits, cries. Brenda just goes to her towel.

"Damn," she said. "Damn damn damn damn damn."

"Why did you say it was shallow?" he says.

They stare at each other, drying off. He does not say, "You saved me," and she does not say, "It was stupid to swim here in the dark."

They go back to the cottage. The others have gone inside. They stay wrapped in their towels and lie in separate chairs. Suddenly they both speak at once.

"I don't know if I'll get out of this country alive," says Nim, and "Maybe you *are* the heaviest man in the world," says Brenda.

We Rented A Rolls and Drove to Disneyland

Mr. Hindley heard his name announced overhead just as he saw the waitress emerging from the kitchen door with what must have been his breakfast. It was eleven o'clock and he hadn't had anything yet. He had been up early but couldn't leave his room because of the telephone; the kids kept calling from Canada. He did not like to take a chance on room service either; yesterday they brought it an hour late, the day before an hour early. He had finally come down here and ordered scrambled egg and bacon, which he knew would hardly count as bacon at all but would be a strip of streaky pork. And now the summons. He knew who it must be. Reluctantly he left his chair at the very moment the waitress set the plate before him.

The tall woman was standing in the centre of the crowded lobby, looking absolutely solid, despite youth and blondness. Hers was a solidity he associated with their part of the world, the part of the world she came from and he still inhabited.

"How do you do?" said Mr. Hindley. He stood three feet away from her, his hands and arms tense, shoulders lifted in a ready position. He cleared his throat.

"Mr. Hindley!" She met his eyes directly and said something about meeting this way. She took his hand. "How are you?"

He nodded. "Better now. I've finally managed to find someone efficient." He attempted a chuckle.

She watched him searchingly. There was a small, still boy with her who had clearly been subjected to this scrutiny himself and understood the need for caution. Mr. Hindley wobbled an eyelid at the boy. The woman seemed to need more.

"I found an international company. Apparently they deal with this sort of thing regularly," he said. "I was just having my breakfast," he said, stepping back a pace. His arm rose halfheartedly in the direction of the coffee shop where the steam must have departed from his longed-for eggs.

"Shall we join you and have a coffee?" she said. She looked down at the boy. "Get you a glass of juice too?"

The coffee shop was decorated with white lattice dividers through which yellow cloth poppies had been wound, ruffled curtains in a brown check, and wicker chairs, creating a depressing effect of homespun Americana. But its windows looked down the circular drive to the Cromwell Road, where eight lanes of morning traffic honked and stalled and sent up noxious fumes into the mist. A chocolate milk-shake and a cup of coffee were being borne in their direction by the waitress in her brown uniform with hat and apron of baby-chick yellow.

Mr. Hindley ate his cool eggs with determination rather than relish.

Jane watched. She had received a telephone call from his daughter in Ottawa at 9:30 this morning, her time, which meant that it was 4:30 a.m. over there.

"So there's my poor dad alone in a London hotel and getting the runaround," Beth had concluded. "Could you get over there and find out what he's doing?"

Jane thought about how she would carry out her assignment. "He was eating his breakfast," she'd say. But it couldn't be let go that easily. His very air of normality made her uneasy.

"You have things under control, then?" She paused. It was the wrong thing to say, a pre-emptive remark. She backed up. "I didn't know there were such international companies."

"They say it happens a lot. You don't think of it but it does." He stopped eating for a moment and looked at her. He had sandy hair and freckles, a ginger mustache, a boyish forward thrust to his chin. "The airline put me on to them, finally. I called them first this morning because I had to make arrangements to get home. The man asked if I would be travelling with Mrs. Hindley."

There was a glint of humour in his eyes. Jane was faintly scandalized. Perhaps this was a reaction to the shock he'd had.

"Last night I was getting the runaround, that's true. I know Beth told you to come. But you see it's all taken care of now. I called the airline, told him what happened, and he gave me a name. 8:30 this morning this was. I called the company. And they're taking charge of it all." He looked triumphant, defiant: no help needed! At the same time he managed to look pathetic.

"Don't, Matthew!" said Jane sharply without turning her head. The boy was lifting the tablecloth to put his car under it.

"Won't do any harm," said Mr. Hindley offhandedly before carrying on. "Last night I just couldn't get anywhere. People kept telling me to call the American Embassy. I don't know what the Americans have to do with it." He gave a wan smile, an appeal to a sensibility he knew they'd both share. Might as well try to amuse her because she'd made the drive out, his tone seemed to say.

"But did you call the Canadian Consulate?"

"They weren't very helpful. They said it was an immigration matter!" He looked at her for a reaction. The chink of coffee cups stopped for a moment.

"Oh!" said Jane. Her face flushed violently. Coffee spilled over the side of her cup. She picked up a serviette and began to mop it up. "But that's mad! Immigration! How could it possibly be?"

Jane groped to understand. There was a lot

of red tape in these matters, but did you really have to immigrate to Britain before you could die here? Pass some kind of test to get in? Perhaps this man's wife had committed an immigration offense by dying on holiday? NO VISA FOR DEMISE: she could see it stamped on those passports for two-week tours. But no, this was Canada's red tape, not Britain's. Did a live Canadian who became dead in Britain have to apply to immigrate to get back home?

In the face of Mr. Hindley's eerie calm, Jane was becoming overwhelmed with the solemnity of her errand. She began to poke the tablecloth with her spoon. Her mind searched frantically for a hold. Was there a department dealing with this final form of migration? Emigration, in fact, to the other shore? A nervous giggle built up in her throat. Mr. Hindley took pity on her.

"He had some kind of English accent," he said. "He wasn't even Canadian." This was offered in part as an excuse for the man's unnatural behaviour, in part as a good-natured criticism. What do we pay our taxes for if not to have people answer telephones in our accent in foreign countries? A less remarkable fellow than Mr. Hindley would have been furious.

"It's happening throughout the foreign service," she said. "They're called 'locally employed.' It's cheaper."

"Oh," said Mr. Hindley. His complaint collapsed before her casual knowledge of such matters. They both looked at Matthew, who was climbing onto the table.

"Perhaps he'd like another milkshake," said Mr. Hindley.

"Yes," said Matthew.

"He's home from school. Supposed to be sick," Jane said.

"It wasn't very big," said Mr. Hindley, displaying another kind of expertise.

"It was NOT BIG," said the child.

"How old are you?"

"Five and a half. I'm going to be five and three quarters soon."

"I have seven grandchildren," said Mr. Hindley. "Ranging in age from twelve to two. And my daughter-in-law is expecting. We were going to Mothercare to buy things for the baby. Yellow is best, is it not?" he turned to Jane, smiling. "When you don't know which it's going to be?"

When he ordered the second milkshake his voice shook.

"You must be terribly tired," said Jane. "Did you sleep?"

"There was a terrific lot of noise in the hall outside my door at three in the morning," he said. "This is not the hotel we normally stay in." Then he added, "I was lucky when they let me stay on."

Preposterous humility, thought Jane. "Well, they wouldn't turn you out in the street!"

"We had already checked out, you see, yesterday morning. Then we went to N. Peal because she wanted to buy me a cashmere sweater. We always got one as a treat in London. They've just about doubled since the last time. Did you know that? But she bought me one anyway. Then we came back to get our bags and we were sitting in the lobby and she said she felt faint."

His eyes were filling now and the red rims growing redder but he kept on with the story. Jane hoped she hadn't pushed him to tell it. "Had your wife been ill?" Jane murmured.

"She never went to doctors," he said, and pushed on. "We sat down and she said don't worry, we'll make the flight. We were on our way to France to stay in the Relais and Châteaux." He said this with a trace of petulance. It gave Jane her first sympathy for Mrs. Hindley. Don't worry, she said, about to die. You'll get your treat.

"We do this every year," Mr. Hindley was saying. "We have an affinity for Europe."

Jane noticed that he had said "we have," in the present tense. But Mr. Hindley didn't correct himself, or notice. He smiled at the mention of their affinity, and kept on talking. "I fought over here, you know. Take every chance I can to get back." His teeth were uneven and stained by nicotine.

"And then the housekeeper came over to see if she could help. Her name was Philippa. It said right on her badge. Well that was odd because it was my wife's name and she never liked it." He swallowed.

"I looked at this badge. I suppose I was confused at first because I thought it meant that she was coming for my wife, you know, like the Angel of Death, with her name on a card. That was when I thought it was getting serious."

Jane was taken with this dramatic quality in the event, and thought how she must tell her husband. A nemesis, the moira, as the Greeks called it: hotel housekeeper bearing wife's own unloved name approaching across the lobby.

"My wife said she felt like she'd been poisoned." He put down his fork. "Apparently it's quite common for people to say this when they are having a heart attack. But perhaps it's why they didn't call an ambulance right away."

The threadbare carpet in the long hallway was brown with gold hexagons. The air smelled stale. Many trays of unfinished meals lay outside doors. In the Hindleys' room were two narrow beds with orange bedspreads, four suitcases and one makeup case. How will he manage with her bags as well? thought Jane. He can't very well leave them.

The room was crowded and ugly, a large television set atop a chest of drawers the only promise of relief. The window overlooked a sidestreet jammed with cars. Mr. Hindley was embarrassed. It was an invasion, for Jane to be there.

He turned on the television for Matthew. Jane called her friend the Deputy High Commissioner. He wasn't there so Jane spoke to the secretary. She relayed the events: a Canadian citizen is here on holiday. His wife has—uh—unfortunately, died, and he called you people. "He was told that it was an immigration matter!" she said with some indignation. "How can this be?" she asked.

The secretary launched in a long bureaucratic answer. It was correct, although there was a misunderstanding. It was a consular matter, sometimes referred to as immigration in a general way because the immigration department is in the consular building. You see this is the High Commission and the consular office is at a different number, and they close at five...

Jane rolled her eyes at Mr. Hindley. He had sat down in a chair in the corner. His arms lay flat on the arm rests and his eyes looked out at her but didn't stop on her, they went on through the thin wall to where noises of cleaning could be heard. At length Jane was put through to a Mr. Couteau, to whom she repeated the tale of Mrs. Hindley's death.

"What has he done so far?" asked the voice in her ear. She told him, repeating the name of the international company.

"They're very reputable," murmured Mr. Couteau. "They dealt with the Air India crash—terrible mess—hundreds of bodies. Don't tell him that," he said with a small cough.

"No, said Jane.

"What did they quote him?"

Jane covered the mouthpiece of the telephone. "Price?" She repeated the price, and Mr. Couteau said that it was reasonable. She asked about the autopsy.

"Standard procedure when a foreigner dies suddenly in Britain."

"What else should we be doing?" she asked. It seemed too quickly wound up.

"They'll do it all. The death certificate will have to be done in the borough, but they'll look after it. The gentleman has done well."

"Right," she said. She hung up the telephone and told Mr. Hindley that he had done well. He seemed satisfied with that.

Matthew had turned off the television and was beginning to make letters on a pad of paper with Mr. Hindley's pen.

"No, Matthew, no. That belongs to Mr. Hindley." She took the piece of paper away.

"I never saw a kid who wouldn't watch television," said Mr. Hindley.

Matthew got up and started to bounce on the bed. He straddled the gap to the twin, fell down, stood up and began bouncing again. It was becoming awkward to remain. Mr. Hindley was standing by the door. He wanted her to go.

"Would you like me to stay with you this afternoon? On your rounds?"

No, he most definitely did not want her to go with him and the efficient international undertaker to get the autopsy report and then to fix up the death certificate. She picked up her coat.

"Beth said you might be a little short of cash," she said. "Because of the travellers' cheques."

Mr. Hindley's eyes veered off to the wall again. He took this as an opportunity to enlarge on he and his wife's travelling finances. "We always get some in each name, but we spent mine first. We always did." He smiled: it had been a petty squabble, in this light a loss. Jane thought of N. Peal and the cashmere sweater. So, Mrs. H., you treated him with his own travellers' cheques, did you? "Now all

I have are in her name and I can't cash them. But I can get cash with my Visa card." His eyes were blank. He was talking but not thinking.

"No, no, that's too expensive."

"Eighteen percent interest," he said. "But there's a new regulation keeping it down. We heard about it on CBC Radio just before we left."

"I went to my bank specially." She pulled a roll of bills out of her purse.

"It really won't be necessary."

Necessary, and a further remoteness in his voice took her back. She held the money awkwardly, afraid to put it out toward him, a man of her father's age. He was embarrassed at being caught in this predicament, the predicament of his wife having died. Jane understood and recognized that state of mind. They were all the same, where they came from. It was a wonder Beth had called to ask for help in the first point. But at this point she wished the rules would collapse, that he would pound his chest in grief, demand pity and succour. It would have been easier for her. But not for Mr. Hindley. He seemed to regard this death as a lapse, a selfish and regrettable outburst, the sooner put down the better.

"When I was first living here my mother died," said Jane. It just slid out, something she never talked about.

"Your mother?" asked Matthew.

"Your grandma. Except you weren't born. Then I met your father. Otherwise I'd probably have gone back," said Jane.

Mr. Hindley did not seem to notice. "The

only thing I'm wondering," he said, as she was leaving, "is how I'm going to get all those suitcases to the airport. When I do manage to get both of us on a flight."

"Beth said you must take cabs. That's why you need cash."

"It's really not necessary," he said again, weakly. He mentioned the taxi driver who'd brought him home from the hospital after he'd left her. He wouldn't let Mr. Hindley pay the fare. "It's the kindness that's the hardest to take," said Mr. Hindley. His eyes filled. Jane thrust the money forward and he took it. His pants were stained. He did not look fresh. It was a nasty hotel room. He wanted her out of there.

Matthew bounded off the bed and out the door. Jane lingered, her hand on the handle. There were three daughters waiting in Canada for her report, three daughters poised to jump on airplanes to come and rescue him.

"Is there anything else I can do?"

"Tell them I'm all right and for God's sake not to come over," he said, vehemently.

"Mummy, where do dead people go?" asked Matthew. They went down the wrong stairs in the hotel and ended up outside the kitchen. They went through some tin swinging doors and jumped off a ledge at a service dock at the back of the hotel.

"They don't go anywhere," Jane said shortly, taking his hand across the street.

"Then why does she need to get on a

plane?"

Jane laughed. "You're too smart for me."

She unlocked the door of the car. The image of Mr. Hindley driving in an undertaker's car across London to sign the death certificate, and trying to book a flight home with his wife's casket when he had been expecting to dine in a French château pursued her across Hyde Park, up through Bayswater to the Edgeware Road. But she pressed ahead, trying to leave behind that burden of grief, mourning, alienation. It was his, after all, not hers.

At home she put on eggs to boil for sandwiches. Matthew got out his cars and sat on the cold basement tiles, murmuring to himself as he slid them up and down the stair. The telephone rang. She heard the clicks that indicated long distance. It was Beth.

"Well, how was he?" Beth said.

"He was eating his breakfast. And he has things under control. He's found an international company."

"What company?"

"Sounded something like Kenyan."

"Oh God," said Beth. "Who knows where she'll end up?" She let out a choked giggle. Jane did too.

"God," said Beth, and "Sorry," said Jane.

What was this instinct to laugh at the death of Philippa Hindley, this unpardonable desire to shriek in hilarity? Was it the vacuum she created, the problems of transporting her box, the strange detachment of her husband? Was it something to do with Beth's mother herself? Jane thought not, although she didn't know her well; the woman was neither heinous nor a saint. But it did seem odd that twenty hours after Philippa's death Jane had not heard a sob nor seen a tear fall. Later she mentioned it to her husband.

"Well, it's because she got off easy," he said. "It's a good death." His own father had two years of painful cancer first. "Setting out on holiday? What could be better?"

"Coming home from it I suppose."

"No, because this way she was looking forward to something."

Wrong, thought Jane savagely, looking at the crown of his head as he bent over some newspaper. Her silent dissent did not make him lift his face, however. You are so afraid of disappointment, she said. Isn't it just like you to want to die with the best still to come?

Looking out the window of the undertaker's car, Mr. Hindley had seen a pub he'd liked the looks of. At the end of the afternoon he went back. Convenient to have Beth's friend's cash: he didn't have to eat in that awful hotel all the time. He got a draught of some live ale or other, probably make him sick but he liked the change.

"Wife died last night," he said to the man next to him. "We're just visiting here."

"Oh, man," said his audience. "That's not good news."

"Well, no, it isn't. And this dying in transit was pretty odd. Just think, in most countries a tourist is an inconvenience when he's living, but when she's dead, forget it."

The man cawed a long laugh. "You said it, buddy, I think you said it."

"And then the girls, you see, it's a bad shock. They weren't thinking about her dying, were they? Just that we were going to be all neatly tucked away in the Relais and Châteaux for the next two weeks. She was not unwell, she didn't go to the doctor, who would have thought?"

The man commiserated again. "You said this just happened yesterday?"

"Course I'm the one, aren't I? She promised we'd do this trip. Here I've got the tickets and I can't even go. Last thing she said, "Don't worry, we'll make the plane to Paris."

"That can throw you off," muttered the other man.

"And when you're travelling the whole thing can be thrown off so easily. It's like I said, sometimes you figure if you take the wrong bus or show up on the wrong day you just get forgotten about. It's almost as if—oh, here we were in London and the ticker didn't get a proper start so too bad."

"I don't follow you there."

"Well, it's not like dying at home. You see, she did the deed in public. Threw me on the mercy of strangers, it did. Didn't have our things around—which I know she'd have wanted. Not the kind of thing she'd have liked to think she was capable of, put it that way," he said. "I feel a bit cheated, that's all."

Seeing he'd lost his audience, Mr. Hindley

called for another beer. It was thick, cold, animated somehow with live organisms; he'd read about this in travel magazines. He put his hand around the glass and felt the possibilities. One thing was for certain and that was Philippa's death set him loose in a wide arc. He felt like a stone that had been pocketed in a sling and the sling whirled around and around. Then without warning the sling was let loose so the stone went off on its own, straight through the air; that was how he would travel now until he lost his momentum and fell.

J ane was clearing up the dishes when the phone rang again.

"It's Bob Hindley," he said.

"Oh yes. How did it go?" She turned her back on Matthew and the radio.

"Autopsy report makes it clear that she died of a massive heart attack, not poisoning," he said. "I don't see how it could have been anyway, we ate all the same things."

Filing the papers in Chelsea with the undertaker they dealt with an official who was having her windows cleaned. He had to spell out the place of birth—"Edmonton, Alberta"—no "w", he always said, because he found that the British put a w on the end of unfamiliar words ending in a. The cleaner stood on a chair and unlocked and washed five multipaned windows, inside and out, before they finished with Mrs. Hindley's details.

"It was impressive," he said.

She thought she was supposed to be

amused, so she chuckled a little at the acuteness of his observation. What was this objectivity? Was it a joke? Was it a complaint? No, it was something else. Mr. Hindley found the combination of sang-froid and cleaning expertise something to remark upon. It was an observation for him to take away from the scene, a little something to offer in the next conversation.

"Are you going to be able to sleep?" she said.

"If the girls would stop phoning from home." There was a little pause. He wanted to say something but found it difficult. "I guess I have to thank you for the fact that they're not coming over. Apparently you told Beth I was okay."

Now they had become conspirators, she and Mr. Hindley. "He was eating his breakfast," Jane had said. What else? She didn't exactly recall. Something about how he really seemed to mean it when she said he didn't want help. She hoped she was right. "I hope you are okay, because if you're not it'll be on me, you know that, don't you?"

He laughed.

"When do you go back?" said Jane.

"Looks like I can get her on a flight with me day after tomorrow," he said.

"What are you going to do until then?"

"I have to pick up the tickets—maybe go to Mothercare..."

"Could we meet for lunch?"

"I don't think that will be necessary," he said.

But now she understood about Mr. Hindley.

"I know it's not necessary," she said firmly. "But I would like it." They settled on the Cafe Royal on Regent Street.

Under the blue-and-gold awning he waited, with his shopping bags. When Jane saw him she thought that, despite the tired pastiness of his face, he looked young, expectant.

They walked through the blood-red bar to the restaurant. In the corner a turbanned Sikh with a waxed mustache smirked over a white piano. "Don't cry for me, Argentina," he mouthed at them. They sat at a white-clothed table in the middle of which were two white carnations sprayed with green paint, in a tiny vase. Oh dear, thought Jane, this is a mistake.

On the wall beside them was a photograph of Kipling, looking young and uncertain, and one of Lord Balfour looking the opposite. Mr. Hindley found the place to his liking. He was fond of trying new places. It was the way he and his wife did France. He and Jane agreed that the best-recommended places are often a disappointment.

"Travelling is more fun when what happens is a surprise."

"To a point," Mr. Hindley said dryly.

Jane looked down at her napkin in alarm. "I'd forgotten about your jokes."

Reaching for the menu, his hand, with liver spots and small ginger hairs sprouting from the knuckles, seemed older than his face. Together they scanned the menu. Mr. Hindley ordered warm duck salad to experiment; Jane only felt like soup and salad.

"And what did you do this morning?" she asked.

He had fixed their tickets to fly back tomorrow to Toronto, where he had to wait four hours for them to transfer his wife to an Ottawa flight. He had to pay fifteen hundred dollars and he got nothing back on his two unused tickets to France and home again. He mentioned these facts without judgement or anger. He went on to say he had purchased all the usual London treats. He'd been to Fortnum and Mason for Easter eggs, to Burberry's and Abercrombie and Fitch. He'd bought the yellow baby things at Mothercare and still planned to go up the street to Hamley's for the grandchildren.

"I don't think they'll mind if you come back without gifts," Jane said.

"Oh no," he said, "I couldn't."

At another table a very loud woman looked familiar to Jane: perhaps she was a gossip columnist. Effortlessly and without ceasing, the theme from *Evita* had become "Puff the Magic Dragon." One beam from the spotlights fell on the table; the others were directed upwards at plaster columns. Each of these columns was a woman naked from the waist up; her head was bowed, her fists pressed to her temples. Trapped in unmoulded plaster from the hip down, the women had no legs. Ambiguously troubled by this condition, they grieved in grace with urns on their heads.

Mr. Hindley liked the ambience. "We have an affinity for Europe," he repeated.

"Considered quite evil in the neighbourhood, don't you recall? We always lived beyond our means." Jane did recall, now, from childhood, some disapproval of the Hindleys for their profligate enjoyment. They were not wealthy, how come they had so much fun? Travelling every summer. The girls in fancy camps.

"Once we rented a Rolls and drove down to Disneyland," he said. "That was in the fifties."

"Oh yes!" cried Jane. Disneyland: Annette Funicello and fabricated Everglades swamps. Parades of singing teenagers with perfect teeth and little boats trailing in circles while dolls of every country revolved before them. How jealous they all had been. So jealous that even the children, in echo of their Depression-era parents, were critical. There was talk that bad fortune must follow the Hindleys. "I do remember."

"We lived on the edge."

Apparently they still did, at seventy. The business with the credit cards, the high interest rates. That would be why Mr. Hindley was so aware. However, at the moment, profligacy looked as if it had been the wise course.

"At least you don't regret"—no, that wasn't it—"At least you made good use of your time."

Mr. Hindley's eyes were small, the lids swollen, the pupils dilated. She didn't even know how he kept his eyes open, after two sleepless nights.

"There's never enough time," he said, coming to attention on her face. "Let this be a lesson to you. Whatever you're waiting for, do it."

As it happened Jane was waiting for a few things. For her hair to grow so she would look more like a certain actress, for Matthew to be older so they could go to art galleries, for her husband to lift his face and look at her. She was waiting to find the perfect studio so she could get some painting done, too. But she didn't much like Mr. Hindley pointing this out. It felt like criticism. Anyway the truth was if she hadn't been waiting for something she'd never have bothered with him and his grief. She wouldn't have been home to receive Beth's phone call in the first place and if she got it she'd have sent around a note like everyone else and that would have been the end of it. Her waiting made her available.

Mr. Hindley did not notice her sudden cooling. He was talking about how they'd come to London when all the girls were under ten and stayed in a bed and breakfast. Five of us in one room, he said. Trekked around to the museums. The kids hated it.

"We," he said, or "my wife and I." He had not mentioned his wife's name since the moment her namesake arrived as nemesis.

The cheque came and Jane picked it up. Mr. Hindley talked on. He seemed to enjoy himself, almost delirious, running through all the premises they'd occupied. A houseboat on the Thames once, for a week, borrowed. As long as he kept her here he was still on his holiday in Europe. He would have this last day despite it all.

London had changed, said Mr. Hindley. Every year it changed but this time they'd particularly noticed. London was becoming more like other places. "McDonalds and what not," he said. "But you live here," he said. "You must like it."

"My husband writes for the stage," she said.

"Beth told me about your husband."

"It's better for him to live here."

Now Mr. Hindley was talking about the play they'd seen in the West End. It wasn't very good. And his wife's wallet had been lifted from her purse in the lobby. But it turned out all right, because they'd gone to the police station and met an American couple who had also been robbed. All four of them had gone for a drink on the coins in his pocket.

"What an awful trip you've had," said Jane, moved past her pique by endless good will.

"It all seems like happy memories now."

"You are a tour agent's dream," she said. "Determined to enjoy."

He dusted his cuffs on the table. "We never had the money but it didn't seem like a reason to miss out on what we liked. I was a civil servant all my life."

"A good life," she said, surmising.

"No," he said. "Take your husband. He could practically write *Death of a Salesman* about me."

"I doubt it," said Jane. It was not clear whether or not this was a comment on her husband's talent as a writer.

Bob Hindley said nothing for a moment.

"If I wrote it you'd come out the hero," said Jane shyly.

A blush mottled his face further. But he did not deny it.

"I'll tell you. This is supposed to be one of the worst things that can happen in life," he said. "That's what the doctor at the hospital told me. For a spouse of fifty years to die like that, so suddenly. Well if this was the worst..." He left the sentence unfinished, for tact, but the thought was completed in the air. *If this is the worst then I won't find the rest impossible by the looks of it.*

"Perhaps you haven't realized it yet."

"Oh, I'm sure it won't sink in until I get back home."

The word "home" rang an ominous note. It was time to go. Jane drew her feet together under the table. Mr. Hindley drank up his third glass of wine. His pupils were so large and black that the pale blue irises had all but disappeared. Jane felt pity for him. The lights had gone out in his house, hadn't they? He would have to adjust to a whole new layout when they went on again. She was just a stranger who chanced to be there when his real life ended, and the denouement began.

They sat in silence, finishing their coffee, thinking about what would happen when he arrived at home. His freedom would be up, the girls would take over.

"I'll be home soon enough," he said. "Got to take my wife back. But what I'm thinking is I won't stay. Oh, the girls will have it all planned for me. Look after this grandchild or that, sell the house, stay with this one or the other. I think they don't really need me and I'll have to branch out. Now don't go telling Beth my plans or you'll ruin it. Look at the bright side. I had a second chance, you know, because I came home from over here alive when most of my buddies were killed. Now I've got a third chance. To make a life."

The pianist was grasping at straws. He had played for hours, now he was on to "Ebb Tide."

Outside the sun had come through and they stood looking at the grand curve of Regent Street.

"I love this place," said Jane suddenly.

"So do I," said Mr. Hindley. He pointed across to Veeraswamy.

"When I come to London again I'm going to try Indian food."

They shook hands. He thanked her very much for all she had done and she said she hadn't done anything really and wished she could have done more. He went up toward Hamley's and she turned down to Piccadilly. And Jane knew with absolute certainty that she would never see Mr. Hindley again.

The Immaculate Conception Photography Gallery

Sandro named the little photography shop on St. Clair Avenue West, between Lord's Shoes and Bargain Jimmies, after the parish church in the village where he was born. He had hankered after wider horizons, the rippled brown prairies, the hard-edged mountains. But when he reached Toronto he met necessity in the form of a wife and babies, and, never having seen a western sunset, he settled down in Little Italy. He photographed the brides in their fat lacquered curls and imported lace, and their quick babies in christening gowns brought over from home. Blown up to near life size on cardboard cutouts, their pictures filled the windows of his little shop.

Sandro had been there ten years already when he first really saw his sign, and the window. He stood still in front of it and looked. A particularly buxom bride with a lace bodice and cap sleeves cut in little scallops shimmered in a haze of concupis- cence under the sign reading Immaculate Concep- tion Photography Gallery. Sandro was not like his neighbours any more, he was modern, a Canadian. He no longer went to church. As he stared, one of the street drunks shuffled into place beside him. Sandro knew them all, they came into the shop in winter. (No one ought to have to stay outside in that cold, Sandro believed.) But he especially knew Becker. Becker was a smart man; he used to be a philosopher at a university.

"Immaculate conception," said Sandro to Becker. "What do you think?"

Becker lifted his eyes to the window. He made a squeezing gesture at the breasts. "I never could buy that story," he said.

Sandro laughed, but he didn't change the sign that year or the next and he got to be forty-five and then fifty and it didn't seem worth it. The Im- maculate Conception Photography Gallery had a reputation. Business came in from as far away as Rosedale and North Toronto, because Sandro was a magician with a camera. He also had skill with brushes and lights and paint, he reshot his nega- tives, he lined them with silver, he had tricks even new graduates of photography school couldn't (or wouldn't) copy.

Sandro was not proud of his tricks. They began in a gradual way, fixing stray hairs and tak- ing wrinkles out of dresses. He did it once, then twice, then people came in asking for it. Perhaps he'd have gone on this way, with small lies, but he met with a situation that was larger than most; it would have started a feud in the old country. During a very large and very expensive wedding party Tony the bridegroom seduced Alicia the bridesmaid in the basketball storage room under the floor of the parish hall. Six months later Tony confessed, hoping perhaps to be released from his vows. But the parents judged it was too late to dissolve the union: Diora was used, she was no longer a virgin, there was a child coming. Tony was reprimanded, Diora consoled, the mothers became enemies, the newlyweds made up. Only Alicia remained to be dealt with. The offence became hers.

In Italy, community ostracism would have been the punishment of choice. But this was Canada, and if no one acknowledged Alicia on the street, if no one visited her mother, who was heavy on her feet and forced to sit on the sofa protesting her daughter's innocence, if no one invited her father out behind to drink home-made wine, Alicia didn't care. She went off to her job behind the till in a drugstore with her chin thrust out much as before. The inlaws perceived that the young woman could not be subdued by the old methods. This being the case, it was better she not exist at all.

Which was why Diora's mother turned up at Sandro's counter with the wedding photos. The pain Alicia had caused! she began. Diora's mother's very own miserable wages, saved these eighteen years, had paid for these photographs! She wept. The money was spent, but the joy was spoiled. When she and Diora's father looked at the row of faces flanking bride and groom there she was—

Alicia, the whore! She wiped her tears and made her pitch.

"You can solve our problem, Sandro. I will get a new cake, we will all come to the parish hall. You will take the photographs again. Of course," she added, "we can't pay you again."

Sandro smiled, it was so preposterous. "Even if I could afford to do all that work for nothing, I hate to say it, but Diora's out to here."

"Don't argue with me."

"I wouldn't be so bold," said Sandro. "But I will not take the photographs over."

The woman slapped the photographs where they lay on the counter. "You will! I don't care how you do it!" And she left.

Sandro went to the back and put his negatives on the light box. He brought out his magic solution and his razor blades and his brushes. He circled Alicia's head and shoulders in the first row and went to work. He felt a little badly, watching the bright circle of her face fade and swim, darken down to nothing. But how easily she vanished! He filled in the white spot with a bit of velvet curtain trimmed from the side.

"I'm like a plastic surgeon," he told his wife. "Take that patch of skin from the inner thigh and put it over the scar on the face. Then sand the edges. Isn't that what they do? Only it isn't a face I'm fixing, it's a memory."

His wife stood on two flat feet beside the sink. She shook the carrot she was peeling. "I don't care about Alicia," she said, "but Diora's mother is making a mistake. She is starting them off with a lie in their marriage. And why is she doing it? For her pride! I don't like this, Sandro."

"You're missing the point," said Sandro.

The next day he had another look at his work. Alicia's shoulders and the bodice of her dress were still there, in front of the chest of the uncle of the bride. He couldn't remove them; it would leave a hole in Uncle. Sandro had nothing to fill the hole, no spare male torsos in black tie. He considered putting a head on top, but whose head? There was no such thing as a free face. A stranger would be questioned, a friend would have an alibi. Perhaps Diora's mother would not notice the black velvet space, as where a tooth had been knocked out, between the smiling faces.

Indeed she didn't but kissed his hand fervently and thanked him with tears in her eyes. "Twenty-five thousand that wedding cost me. Twenty-five thousand to get this photograph and you have rescued it."

"Surely you got dinner and a dance too?" said Sandro.

"The wedding was one day. This is forever," said Diora's mother.

"I won't do that again," said Sandro, putting the cloth over his head and looking into his camera lens to do a passport photo. In the community the doctored photograph had been examined and re-examined. Alicia's detractors enjoyed the headless shoulders as evidence of a violent punishment.

"No, I won't do that again at all," said Sandro

to himself, turning aside compliments with a shake of his head. But there was another wedding. After the provolone e melone, the veal picata, the many-tiered cake topped with swans, the father of the bride drew Sandro aside and asked for a set of prints with the groom's parent's removed.

"My God, why?" said Sandro.

"He's a bastard. A bad man."

"Shouldn't have let her marry his son, then," said Sandro, pulling a cigarette out of the pack in his pocket. These conversations made him nervous.

The father's weathered face was dark, his dinner-jacket did not button around his chest. He moaned and ground his lower teeth against his uppers. "You know how they are, these girls in Canada. I am ashamed to say it, but I couldn't stop her."

Sandro said nothing.

"Look, I sat here all night long, said nothing, did nothing. I don't wanna look at him for the next twenty years."

Sandro drew in a long tube of smoke.

"I paid a bundle for this night. I wanna remember it nice-like."

The smoke made Sandro nauseous. He dropped his cigarette and ground it into the floor with his toe, damning his own weakness. "So what am I going to do with the table?"

The father put out a hand like a tool, narrowed his eyes, and began to saw, where the other man sat.

"And leave it dangling, no legs?"

"So make new legs."

"I'm a photographer, not a carpenter," said Sandro. "I don't make table legs."

"Where you get legs is your problem," said the father. "I'm doing well here. I've got ten guys working for me. You look like you could use some new equipment."

And what harm was it after all, it was only a photograph, said Sandro to himself. Then too there was the technical challenge. Waiting until they all got up to get their bonbonnière, he took a shot of the head table empty. Working neatly with his scalpel, he cut the table from this second negative, removed the inlaws and their chairs from the first one, stuck the empty table-end onto the table in the first picture, blended over the join neatly, and printed it. Presto! Only one set of inlaws.

"I don't mind telling you, it gives me a sick feeling," said Sandro to his wife. "I was there. I saw them. We had a conversation. They smiled for me. Now..." he shrugged. "An empty table. Lucky I don't go to church any more."

"Let the man who paid good money to have you do it confess, not you," she said. "A photograph is a photograph."

"That's what I thought too," said Sandro.

The next morning Sandro went to the Donut House, got himself a take-out coffee and stood on the street beside his window.

"Why do people care about photographs so much?" he asked Becker. Becker had newspaper stuffed in the soles of his shoes. He had on a pair of stained brown pants tied up at the waist with a paisley necktie. His bottle was clutched in a paper bag gathered around the neck.

"You can put them on your mantle," said Becker. "They don't talk back."

"Don't people prefer life?" said Sandro.

"People prefer things," said Becker.

"Don't they want their memories to be true?"

"No," said Becker.

"Another thing. Are we here just to get our photograph taken? Do we have a higher purpose?"

Becker pulled one of the newspapers out of his shoe. There were Brian and Mila Mulroney having a gloaty kiss. They were smeared by muddy water and depressed by the joint in the ball of Becker's foot.

"I mean real people," said Sandro. "Have we no loyalty to the natural?"

"These are existential questions, Sandro," said Becker. "Too many more of them and you'll be out here on the street with the rest of us."

Sandro drained the coffee from his cup, pitched it in the bin painted "Keep Toronto Clean" and went back into his gallery. The existential questions nagged. But he did go out and get the motor drive for the camera. In the next few months he eradicated a pregnancy from a wedding photo, added a daughter-in-law who complained of being left out of the Christmas shots, and made a groom taller. Working in the dark-room, he was hit by vertigo. He was on a slide, beginning a descent. He wanted to know what the bottom felt like.

After a year of such operations a man from the Beaches came in with a tiny black and white photo of a long-lost brother. He wanted it coloured and fitted into a family shot around a picnic table on Centre Island.

"Is this some kind of joke?" said Sandro. It was the only discretion he practised now: he wanted to talk about it before he did it.

"No. I'm going to send it to Mother. She thinks Christopher wrote us all off."

"Did he?" said Sandro.

"Better she should not know."

Sandro neglected to ask if Christopher was fat or thin. He ended up taking a medium-sized pair of shoulders from his own cousin and propping them up behind a bush, with Christopher's head on top. Afterward, Sandro lay sleepless in his bed. Suppose that in the next few months Christopher should turn up dead, say murdered. Then Mother would produce the photograph stamped Immaculate Conception Photography Gallery, 1816 St. Clair Avenue West. Sandro would be implicated. The police might come.

"I believe adding people is worse than taking them away," he said to his wife.

"You say yes to do it, then you do it. You think it's wrong, you say no."

"Let me try this on you, Becker," said Sandro the next morning. "To take a person out is only half a lie. It proves nothing except that he was not in that shot. To add a person is a whole lie: it proves that he was there, when he was not."

"You haven't proven a thing, you're just fooling around with celluloid. Have you got a buck?" said Becker.

"It is better to be a murderer than a creator. I am playing God, outplaying God at His own game." He was smarter than Becker now. He knew it was the photographs that lasted, not the people. In the end the proof was in the proof. Though he hadn't prayed in thirty years, Sandro began to pray. It was like riding a bicycle: he got the hang of it again instantly. "Make me strong," he prayed, "strong enough to resist the new equipment that I might buy, strong enough to resist the temptation to expand the gallery, to buy a house in the suburbs. Make me say no to people who want alterations."

But Sandro's prayers were not answered. When people offered him money to dissolve an errant relative, he said yes. He said yes out of curiosity. He said yes out of a desire to test his skills. He said yes out of greed. He said yes out of compassion. "What is the cost of a little happiness?" he said. "Perhaps God doesn't count photographs. After all, they're not one of a kind."

Sandro began to be haunted, in slow moments behind the counter in the Immaculate Conception, by the faces of those whose presence he had tampered with. He kept a file—Alicia the lusty bridesmaid, Antonia and Marco, the undesired inlaws. Their heads, their shoes and their hands, removed from the scene with surgical precision, he saved for the moment when, God willing, a forgiving relative would ask him to replace them. But the day did not come. Sandro was not happy.

"Becker," he said, for he had a habit now of buying Becker a coffee first thing in the morning and standing out if it was warm, or in if it was cold, for a chat. "Becker, let's say it's a good service I'm doing. It makes people happy, even if it tells lies."

"Sandro," said Becker, who enjoyed his coffee, "these photographs, doctored by request of the subjects, reflect back the lives they wish to have. The unpleasant bits are removed, the wishes are added. If you didn't do it, someone else would. Memory would. It's a service."

"It's also money," said Sandro. He found Becker too eager to make excuses now. He liked him better before.

"You're like Tintoretto, painting in his patron, softening his greedy profile, lifting the chin of his fat wife. It pays for the part that's true art."

"Which part is that?" said Sandro, but Becker didn't answer. He was still standing there when Diora came in. She'd matured, she'd gained weight, and her twins, now six years old, were handsome and strong. Sandro's heart flew up in his breast. Perhaps she had made friends with Alicia, perhaps Diora had come to have her bridesmaid reinstated.

"The long nightmare is over," said Diora. "I've left him."

The boys were running from shelf to shelf lifting up the photographs with their glass frames and putting them down again. Sandro watched them with one eye. He knew what she was going to say.

"I want you to take him out of those pictures," she said.

"You'd look very foolish as a bride with no groom," he said severely.

"No, no, not those," she said. "I mean the kids' birthday shots."

They had been particularly fine, those shots, taken only two weeks ago, Tony tall and dark, Diora and the children radiant and blonde.

"Be reasonable, Diora," he said. "I never liked him myself. But he balances the portrait. Besides, he was there."

"He was not there!" cried Diora. Her sons went on turning all the pictures to face the walls. "He was never there. He was running around, in his heart he was not with me. I was alone with my children."

"I'll take another one," said Sandro. "Of you and the boys. Whenever you like. This one stays like it is."

"We won't pay."

"But Diora," said Sandro, "everyone knows he's their father."

"They have no father," said Diora flatly.

"It's immaculate conception," said Becker gleefully.

But Diora did not hear. "It's our photograph, and we want him out. You do your job. The rest of it's none of your business." She put one hand on the back of the head of each of her twins and marched them out the door.

Sandro leaned on his counter idly flipping the pages of a wedding album. He had a vision of a great decorated room, with a cake on the table. Everyone had had his way, the husband had re-

moved the wife, the wife the husband, the bridesmaid her parents, and so forth. There was no one
there.

"We make up our lives out of the people
around us," he said to Becker. "When they don't
live up to standard, we can't just wipe them out."

"Don't ask me," said Becker. "I just lit out
for the streets. Couldn't live up to a damn thing."
Then he too went out the door.

"Lucky bugger," said Sandro.

Alone, he went to his darkroom. He opened
his drawer of bits and pieces. His disappeared ones,
the inconvenient people. His body parts, his halves
of torsos, tips of shiny black shoes. Each face, each
item of clothing punctured him a little. He looked at
his negatives stored in drawers. They were scarred,
pathetic things. I haven't the stomach for it, not any
more, thought Sandro.

As he walked home, St. Clair Avenue
seemed very fine. The best part was, he thought,
there were no relationships. Neither this leaning
drunk nor that window-shopper was so connected to
any other as to endanger his, or her, existence. The
tolerance of indifference, said Sandro to himself, trying to remember it so that he could tell Becker.

But Sandro felt ill at ease in his own home,
by its very definition a dangerous and unreliable
setting. His wife was stirring something, with her
lips tight together. His children, almost grown up
now, bred secrets as they looked at television. He
himself only posed in the doorway, looking for hidden seams and the faint hair-lines of an airbrush.

That night he stood exhausted by his bed.

His wife lay on her side with one round shoulder above the sheet. Behind her on the wall was the photo he'd taken of their village before he left Italy. He ought to reshoot it, take out that gas station and clean up the square a little. His pillow had an indentation, as if a head had been erased. He slept in a chair.

In the morning he went down to the shop. He got his best camera and set up a tripod on the sidewalk directly across the street. He took several shots in the solid bright morning light. He locked the door and placed the CLOSED sign in the window. In the darkroom he developed the film, floating the negatives in the pungent fluid until the row of shop fronts came through clearly, the flat brick faces, the curving concrete trim, the two balls on the crowns. Deftly he dissolved each brick of his store, the window and the sign. Deftly he reattached each brick of the store on the west side to the bricks of the store to the east.

I have been many things in my life, thought Sandro, a presser of shutters, a confessor, a false prophet. Now I am a bricklayer, and a good one. He taped the negatives together and developed them. He touched up the join and then photographed it again. He developed this second negative and it was perfect. Number 1812, Lord's Shoes, joined directly to 1820, Bargain Jimmies: the Immaculate Conception Photography Gallery at 1816 no longer existed. Working quickly, because he wanted to finish before the day was over, he blew it up to two feet by three feet. He cleared out his window display of brides and babies and stood up this new photograph—one of the finest he'd ever taken, he thought. Then he took a couple of cameras and a bag with the tripod and some lenses. He turned out the light, pulling the door shut behind him, and began to walk west.